THE LAST OF HER PEOPLE

THE WILDS

JESS M. ROSE

If there's a book that you want to read, but it hasn't been written yet, then you must write it.

— Toni Morrison

PROLOGUE

When I wake up, my bed is cold. My fingers stretch out, seeking the comfort that I have always longed for; the warmth that my siblings find with our mama and our papa. Nothing. I am alone. I sleep by myself in a small grass made hut with charms adorning the outside meant to protect others from the despised and the wicked. For I was born wicked.

My name is Ara Macao, for my mama wished to call me something that was not so evil hoping it would rub off on me— she was wrong. She named me after the people of our village, the Ara Macao. Hoping the spirit of the colorful birds, the wings of our ancestors would push away the dark skin and fur that I was born with.

And demon eyes that I cannot change.

The Ara Macao people have always been prosperous. We lived together and we trade for the betterment of our peoples. The trees are rich with colorful birds for which our people named themselves after and how we became so decadent in our trades. For every tribe wanted the feathers of the holy spirits so they could have fortune and make sure the departed souls had wings for flight.

From around the world, the strange traders from the waters came. Their pale eyes and skin unlike anything we have ever seen except for the faces of our name sake. The Ara Macao. Some of these traders had red hair and facial fur like the color of the birds though their skin a motley color of reds and pale flesh beneath their fine clothe. They interested us for their differences, and they seemed equally curious of ours. The feathers we adorned and the animals that we could bring them. More importantly, I think, they continued to come back to us not for furs or the feathers of our names but for the shiny and colorful rocks that our peoples traded in. We had something that they wanted, and they had something we desired.

Their soft cloth was like the down from the red birds but paler and better suited to be worn on the flesh. It protected from the sun and the winds and the cold. They had offered strange medicines and foods, but our people did not need those. Our ancestors protected us. We were the symbol of the blessed for the birds roosted above us. We did not need their strange looking tapir with the short legs and nose that dripped wet. We did not need the small white, brown and red birds they ate. The trees provided everything we needed. When the trees failed, the waters of the sea and shore gave us supper. What we wanted was what they wore. The traders from the waters learned to brings only clothing and some tools for trade. In return, they got our rocks. Beautiful symbols of the stars and the deep fathoms of the sky, but they were only just rocks.

I am Ara Macao of the Ara Macao people and I have shamed

myself and that of my family, though I know not what I have done or how I did it. They say I threw my dark and evil spirit at one of these traders from the waters. He fell down the cliff and died. His people claimed we cast a demon in the shape of a large black puma at them before it vanished into the coal of their fires, extinguishing the flames. That was ten years ago, and I was only five years old.

The traders had not come since. Though we still think upon those times with great joy. A fond memory that can never be again, shared over the fire when the shaman tells the stories `of the past. I am no longer welcomed to those fires, though I hear from my cot the words that he speak. Of an evil spirit that cannot be killed less it take the lives of the killers. I am safe for now. I think they fear me almost as much as I fear myself. Our people blame me for that man's death.

My mama adorned me since my birth in reds, yellows and blues of the colorful bird of our ancestors, to make the evil within me go away. She believed it had worked until that man died. She tried harder and the people of the village demanded of my family that I be removed and have the spells put over my sleeping soul at night so that the demon within me would not wander and kill as it had so long ago. They believed it would work. My mama believed it would work. They were wrong.

1

There is a chill in the air. I pull the cobija up to my chin, longing for the comfort of sleep. The comfort of a companion. Here, I am alone but in my dreams there is a friend. The only one that would deign to talk with me happens to be the one the people are afraid of.

I had once told my mama and papa about the spirit walker in my dreams.

"Shhhh," my mama had said to me. "You must not talk of such things. You are different, my child. You must take care."

"You protect her too much. Let her find out what happens to those that talk to evil spirits."

My mama always tried to comfort and protect me. She would leap over a running water and face the water spirits wrath, all for me. My papa, he was more stern than she. He did not fear the evil spirits like the rest of the people. He would raise a hand to me if I showed him disrespect, and he faced the evil within me every time he did so. I feared for him in those moments even when I hated him.

Physical punishment was not the way of our people. Not to children or those unmarried. The traders from the waters showed us a different way and our people adapted to them. I do not think my father hates me. He truly believes that he can beat the demon out of me. My screams and cries could silence the village. And at night, deep within the forest, the panther roared its anger. It promised retribution. And spirits do not lie. So, I avoid him, too.

"Ara Macao!" My mama yells from the family tent. "Ara Macao!"

I prop myself up on one elbow. There is enough light in the small cot to see the outline of each thicket and grass sewn together with mud and finely trimmed foliage. I remove myself from my bed, it sways gently from the ceiling. It looked like how I felt on most mornings; limp, lifeless with my body in it.

I hear my mama still calling for me.

"I hear you mama," I call out to her, rubbing at my face with the palms of my hands. "I am up."

"The birds are up before you!"

"They are always up before me!" It was true. The loud raucous caws of the red birds of our name sake were up before the sun rose. Loud and demanding. Just like my mother.

"The men have gone to find food. Come, we must prepare for their return!"

The men. The warriors. Though they were not truly warriors any longer. They were hunters. Gone for hours at a time, sometimes days. Food was always nearby for our people, but the men liked to try themselves against the spirit walkers; animals born much larger than their brethren.

Removing the grass barrier and easing myself out from the small aperture I provided for myself. I always did these little things. Things I liked to test myself against. Small openings to tread through. Walking on stone. Climbing trees. Swinging from branches. And always I follow a path. If I deter, I have to rewind myself. These little quirks drove my family mad.

I step from my lonely little cot and out into the morning ambience. The forest was all around us. We live on a small hill of rock and stone, if you stand on the precipice you will just about see the ocean where the traders used to come. The giant white wings of the birds they sailed upon could be seen from there.

"Ara Macao!" My mother calls again.

"I'm coming." I mutter into my palm, stifling a yawn as I squat behind my cot to make water. It is considered rude to yawn and a bad omen. Children and the very old are given leniencies for their spirits were not bound to their bodies. I am not given such leniencies. It is said that if you yawned and close your eyes, a demon could possess your body. If you sneezed with your eyes open—your soul was already gone. Something about the exhalation of breath allowing for the deep fathoms to take hold of you. And in my case, it did not look good.

The family homes are not far from my dwellings. The clearing up ahead held the shabonos, each conical in shape, with thatched palm leaves and wood, surrounded by an open space where the young children could roam and play as the old watches them from the comfort of soft ferns and grasses. Not far from them would be where the older girls, young women and mothers would cut fruits and vegetation. Preparing the ground with rocks for fire. Later, the women will check over the homes to make sure they are weatherproofed. Then we would weave and craft. Some of us were permitted to fish if the men were gone for too long.

"There you are, Ara Macao." The soft voice of my grandmother spoke. "She has been asking for you, child. Your feet been in running water?"

"No grandmama," I say. "I was asleep."

"You sleep for too long. You must be careful. Only the spirits sleep like you do." Grandmama gave me a piercing look over her face of sagacity. Long grey and white hairs fell from her head, speaking of her years of wisdom.

"Yes, grandmama." I brush away my thick curls from my face with the back of my hand.

"That is a good child," she says gently, reaching out a hand to caress my face. She was the only one who touched me, now. Though she was always careful not to be seen doing so. "Now go to your father. Maybe later I will tell you a story." Grandmama has amazing stories. The shaman did not like her speaking the stories of when she was a child. For she remembered when he was a little boy.

Sunfather's light was warm on my skin as I walk to where my mama would be. The dank odor of the old fire pit and the previous night's meal blended with the fragrances and the smell of the early morning—and fresh melon!

"Mama, I have come to help you prepare the meals."

"Aye-e-e! There you are you bad girl." Mama did not look pleased. She was not alone. The other mothers of the village and the ones not yet with children of their own, glowered at me as I entered the area. They tended to their tasks of weaving grasses into baskets, creating garments, cutting and stripping dry foliage.

"Something smells."

Oh no…

"It's our little sister."

I close my eyes, dreading the two who spoke.

Kali and Keira, my older sisters both born of the same womb, their soul split into separate bodies upon birth. They have been a bane in my existence since I was born.

"You are supposed to be helping your sisters with the baskets." My mama was cutting open fresh melon. The fresh aroma of sweet fruit draws me towards her.

"I hate weaving!" I say. "Why does everyone wake up before SunFather's has the chance to heat the ground?" I take a chance and grab for a slice of the tender fruit.

Success! My hand squeezes around the fruit, sweet liquid flowing between my fingers as I draw back with my prize. My mama turned to me and raises her hand—but she is not like my father who hits me or my grandmama who secretly touches my cheek. Her hand falls to her side, and she sighs with defeat. "You bad child."

"Stupid sister."

"Bad sister."

Even now I cannot tell them apart. If I am the one born with a wicked spirit, then I do not know what to call these two. I glower at them and stick out my tongue, it is covered in fruit and they make faces of disgust at me.

"You need to grow up," Keira says, holding a finger to her nose as if a foul smell had entered the area. A wooden lizard was clipped to her hair, keeping her dark tresses from falling into her face.

"You shame us with your childish behavior," Kali says, like her sister, she wears a wooden turtle in a neat plait. Her eyes met her sisters and then her hand, too, went to her nose.

"I am hungry—I have the right to food." I shove the rest of fruit into my mouth before anyone has the chance to take it from me. I have learned in the past that if it's not eaten quickly, whatever it is might be taken away. "Are we cooking maize?"

"Only when you have worked for it do you deserve to eat," Kali says.

"We have been up with the birds. We have done our obligation to the people. What have you done but sleep in?"

"I stay up late doing what you do during the day." I lick my lips and then my fingers, tasting the remnants of the delicious fruit. I want more but know that if I try to take another piece mama might touch me—I do not want that. Nobody does.

"You would not need to stay up late, Ara Macao, if you rose with the SunFather's."

I cross my arms. And saw that this confrontation had attracted the notice of the other women in the village. Pia, Tuli, Ava, Okalaki, Tosha, Zashi, and all the rest from my age to my mother's age. They all stared at me with disapproving frowns. What have I done?

"This is why you have not found a man," the voice of Tosha says. She is a tall woman, almost as tall as me. She was as light as the moon as I was dark from the sun. Her hair brown and lush, her eyes a burnish copper. I heard whispers that her mother might have lain with one of the traders that had come so long ago. "If you knew how to bathe and clean yourself and behave like a woman, you might have become pregnant by now."

"Babies? Who are you to talk to me about babies?" I snap. They are always against me in everything. Many of them did not know what they were talking about and only disliked me because I was different. "Tosh-Tosh-Tosha. Why are you not pregnant? Maybe whatever it is you are doing is frowned upon by the spirits!"

Her cheeks flare a pretty red. "You are an animal!" Tosha growls, tossing her hair over her shoulder. Even when angry she was beautiful, and I envy her of that. She storms away, her hips swaying prettily. She had rounded out in all the right parts since getting joined with a man. She had carried babes, twice in the last eighteen months but each time the child had not been born with her mate's spirit animals' guidance. The children had been birthed too early, not surviving the night. Each time, the water spirits had taken the body, to carry it out to sea to the horizon where the sky and the sea finally meet. The sea out there, where the traders on wings of giant birds, used to sail.

It is said that when a woman could not conceive a man's seed, that she secretly harbors a spirit animal which covets her attention and dispels the child. Cruel things to think about but then again it is Tosha. Vile woman.

Guilt floods me and I turn, raising my hand to stop her flight. "Tosha, wait, I—"

"Leave her alone, spirit walker!" Okalaki says, standing to confront me. She was not a small woman and had born four babies consecutively with each baby growing fat and healthy. And most of all, living to see their third naming day.

"At least she does not have the black puma walking in her

shadow!" Tuli throws a coconut shell at me and I duck before it hits me. It sails through the air, right where I had been standing just a moment ago.

"Ara Macao—go to the water. Bring fresh water." Mama whispers in shame. I can see fresh tears running down her face. But does she see mine? No, she does not even raise her head to look at me.

"Go and bathe!" Kali says fingering the wooden turtle adorning the end of her braid.

"Then bring back fresh water," Keira says, her hands on her hips.

"Nothing can stop the stink of that one," Okalaki says. "She smells like a black panther."

"As if she has a spirit animal," another voice chimes in. It is the short Zosha.

The people fall into silence as if waiting for me to address their accusations. I do not give into their bullying and I make my hasty retreat grateful that the shaman was not around.

2

———

As soon as I'm back in the trees, I pass my cot, and retrieve my bow and sheath or arrows from the log nearby. I pull up my hunting knife that was much larger than the ones the women carry. Women were not allowed to have such weapons. We are allowed to carry our carving knives; knives meant to shear wood, branch and leaves, stripping them and apply them to craft. We are allowed to use knives to cut fruits and to tend to meat pits. Only men could carry a bow and arrow. Only men could carry a hunting knife. And I was not allowed to have any of it.

And so, I stole mine and hid them in secret.

Women were cherished. Presumed too soft to venture too far into the woods, alone. Monsters lay in these woods. Spirit animals much larger than their living brethren. They wanted a person to bond with, so the men go out and bond with them in how men do. With their bow and their arrow. With their hunting knives. It was a great sport. They would not eat the flesh of such an animal—that would be evil. But the one who bonded with the beast would wear its protective skin and the animal will help guide them in their life and to their next.

Even though the forest was off limits for the women to adventure alone, I was not given that prohibition. I sometimes will see a few of the women come out to these woods, together. Cutting fruit from trees to collecting palm nuts and sweet berries and I will sometimes want that. The companionship of another woman. A friend.

Sometimes, the shaman says it will be all right for the women to hold spears, we can all go to the river, together, and use the spears to hunt for fish. Most of the women are not very good, and I suspect it is a joke that the shaman took great pleasure in seeing them fumble and foil about. Though I never do. I think the women hate me for that, too.

I picked up my handmade spear as I make my way to the river—not the area where all the women would come to when collecting water—this was an area that the others have never been to. Only the bold would venture down the river where animals and the other forest dwellers might find them. Though the peoples of the forest traded, we were all rivals. Some less civil, less willing to be friendly. Sometimes death did happen because someone broke the boundaries. That was a thing of men.

Unlike the other women of my village, I could hold my own. I was certain of that.

And yet, if the men fail to come back the same day they leave, the women and children might go hungry. There have been years when we have to venture further and further out for our fruits and our palm nuts. I remember being hungry and going into the woods. Nobody would stop me. When I came back with food, nobody would eat what I touched.

The shaman did not give his blessing to hunt the fish in the river. There had been a time when the women did not listen to the shaman, and one year a sudden flood had taken the lives of five women. Their children orphaned because the mothers had not listened. That is an older story—it had not happened since I have been born. Probably a story to keep the women in check. Well, I say to that, we shall see.

The river was wide, it would take almost twenty holding hands to cross it. In the weeping season, when the stars cried, the river would be much larger. More dangerous. Right now, as the sun hits my back, as the mud of the bank squishes between my toes and fingers, it is safe. Except for the few predators that lurk around.

I lean toward the water, counting the fish swimming by. All too small for a spear to pierce. I grab a few round rocks and play with them between my fingers. It feels good. Another one of my weird quirks. My more common quirk. Rolling rocks between my palm and my fingers.

"What do you think you're doing here?" A familiar voice says from over my shoulder.

I almost spook, and fall forward, my arms bracing me before I fall face first into the water. My sudden movement scaring the fish away from the bank. I round on the forest boy. Banu. He is like me. My only friend in this world. Dark skinned, hair so thick it looks like fur growing on his arms and chest. Dark mane going down his back.

His eyes, like my own.

Green.

"What are you doing here?" I ask him. "You scared away all the fish. Now I will need to move and find a new spot to catch meat."

"There are large caimans in these waters. You should take care, Ara Macao." He says my name with the roll of amusement on his tongue. I can see he is trying to aggravate me into doing something.

"Do not test me, forest boy. I have had a rough morning."

"Gotten into a fight again?" He asks, taking a seat next to me, his legs pulled up to his chin. With his face in his hands and his hands on his legs, he looked outrageously stupid looking at me like that.

I shove him and his ridiculous face. As he tumbles over, I stand to look down at him. "I do not start fights. It's like they want me to fight them, to see me fail, or something. They are happy in my unhappiness."

"Sounds like a typical female," Banu says as he rises to his feet. His legs are dirty from the riverbank. "But you smell like a monkey. You should bathe more often."

"And you? Look at you, Banu. You're covered in filth, like a sloth. Is that lichen that I see growing in your hair?"

His hand reaches up to the top of his head, patting the matts and tangles and I chuckle at him. He has a way to make his matted hair look natural. Intended. As his eyes met mine, he lowers his hand. There was a cunning in his eyes, the look of someone who is far too smart for their own good. And his eyes were on mine. They look very warm and inviting.

He smiles ruefully. "Want to go for a swim?"

"I thought you just said there are caiman in the river?"

"There are always caimans in the river."

"I don't want to die, you idiot." I sigh and look into the water longingly. "I was told to bathe and then fetch the water for my people. I don't think I can stay and play with you today."

This time that awful smile spreads across his face. The smile that makes my legs feel weak. "I know of a spring nearby. If you wish to bathe."

I chuckle and shake my head at his audacity. "Maybe later. I think someone else can go and fetch the water. My people need meat. The men have just left. I do not think they will come back anytime soon."

Banu shrugs. He never liked talking about the hunters that wandered into the forest, searching for meat, or spirits to bond. I look at him and frown.

"Have they spotted you?" My face crunches up with concern until he shakes his head.

"No, they do not realize that I am here. I hide very well."

"I wish my people did not realize I was here, too." I wish I could bite back those words. I do not think they were true and by the look Banu gave me, he did not think so either, but he was kind enough to let it slide. He knows how much I long for the recognition and the respect of the men and women of the village. To be part of something.

"Do you want to hunt, then?" he asks.

"I would like that.

He holds out his hand. I stare at it and smile up at him. A small smile tugging at the corner of his mouth. He was such a trickster. I shove him aside and run ahead of him. "Come, Banu. Let us find some meat. I am hungry!"

3

When I was younger, I scared my older sisters to death, the things I would blurt out about my dreams and the spirit animal that haunted them—and of seeing someone lurking in the forest at night. Eventually I understood that this would only lead to more fright from the villagers and complete shunning if it continues. They think me a demon.

And they are probably right.

I was the only one with a night watcher lurking in my dreams. A spirit animal that would take a wandering soul to the starless fathoms of the sky, away from our ancestors. And I was the only one to know of the forest boy.

Learning to hold my tongue about my dreams and of the forest boy had been difficult. After my sixth birthday, when I had first seen the child in the woods, I had reported it to my people. First to my papa and then to my mama. They were still angry with me about the previous year's incident, but they were concerned that one child had become lost in the woods. All the village had been made aware of it and yet all the children were made accountable.

The shaman issued the warriors to find this wandering child, "Don't touch him when you find him, less he is a night watcher in disguise of a boy! Burn fire and create smoke, the demons will flee!" Adorned in charms, that is what they did. Running past the small hut that had been prepared just for me, adorned in trinkets that they wore like bijou the traders often wore. Well into the night they searched with their fires and their holy protection. They came back looking tired. Haggard. And angry.

I had been shunned for almost a month. A long and hard month for one of five years to endure. I had missed my mama and papa's warmth, the laughter of my eldest sisters despite the cruel pokes and jabs they did. Sometimes they would pull my fur on my arms and make me cry only to see the tears fall. Yet I missed them. Most would not have survived.

Papa is unaware of my mama's help during that time. How I cried and begged for the people to see me to only have them turn away and look into the air, never once looking me in the eyes. I stomped. I begged. I even threw the food around. Not one saw me.

I went off into the woods for I knew the forest boy could see me.

"Why do they ignore you, little sister?" He had asked me.

"They did not believe me."

"They came into the woods to find me. I did not let them see me."

"Why not?" I remember crying as I leaned up against him. He wasn't even much older than I was. "Now I am all alone."

"You are not alone," he said to me. "I am here, just like you."

"You are the only one who is nice to me. I am sorry I told the people about you. I only want friends. I thought maybe you could live with me."

"I will be your friend," he said into my ear as his warm arms wrapped around me. "But I cannot live in the village. I am a forest boy."

"What is a forest boy?"

"One who lives in the forest," he said, before shoving me backwards into the water.

I came up coughing and sputtering but the tears had been washed away from my face and an anger burned beneath the sadness. I jumped on him, my fingers out like claws.

"You could become a forest girl," he said, his hands raised before his face protectively.

"And be all wet and muddy, like you? Now, I stink."

"You already smell," he admitted.

I did smack him then. Then I rose to my feet, covered in grasses and mud, but feeling much better about myself, even though I had just been told that I stank. I held out my hand, and the forest boy takes my hand and I helped him to his feet. Then the next thing I know, I was flying backwards back into the water that I had just crawled out from!

"You are so bad!" I yelled at him.

"Come and live with me!" He looks ready to pounce on me.

I take a reed that is growing in the water and brandish it like a weapon. "In the forest? I am not an animal!"

Suddenly, he jumps, landing in the water before me. I am shocked and I lower my hand with my weapon. As he surfaces, he throws back his hair and looks me in the eyes.

"I can teach you about the forest. Make you stronger."

I looked at him skeptically. He was not much older than me, only a few years my senior and I was already finding myself looking up to him like a role model.

"Why do you wear red feathers?" he suddenly asked me.

I startled, forgetting that I was wearing the feather necklace my mama had made for me to keep the ancestor spirits with me. "To keep the demons away," I answered, running a finger over the wet feather.

"Why would that keep demons away?"

I puzzled at the question before answering. "Red signifies blood. Blood of our ancestors. There are more stars in the sky then there is darkness. Together we are strong, alone we are weak. The feathers represent a power of blood that binds us and the bond we have with our ancestors. They protect us."

He looked skeptical. I glared at him for how he doubted my mamas' words and the gift she had given me to keep me safe. "They look like something to play with." That is what he believed? I was shocked and a little angry.

"They are holy and offer protection!"

"Well, they will only get in the way. That, or break and become ruined. They're too pretty to be broken."

I fingered the feathers fondly and feel fresh tears bud at the corner of my eyes.

"Put that on the riverbank," he says as he points to the scarlet feather necklace, "and let your mama find it. Come with me, and I'll show you how to live for the month you are not allowed to be with your family."

"You will truly protect me?" I asked of him.

He took a step closer to me and touched the feather

necklace before meeting my eyes. "I will protect you more than those feathers can."

I hesitated a moment longer before moving away from him. He did not make to follow. Only I could make this decision and I had decided. I moved towards the bank, feeling the soft mud underfoot. Back then my mind did not consider how dangerous these waters could be with their underwater predators. I turned back to the boy. He had not moved.

He seemed to be waiting.

I had made my decision. I removed the necklace and put it onto the riverbank before turning back to the forest boy. The only person in the entire world who treated me like a person who spoke to me, who did not fear my touch. And better than anything in the world, he looked like me.

"What is your name?" I asked him as I stepped up to him. He began to move backwards, going deeper into the water that I had no other choice but to follow. The water of the river pushing against my waist. I had never been in the water this deep before.

The water was up to my chest as he spoke, "It is only courtesy to say your name first."

As the water touched my neck and my feet began to push off from the ground, fear finally began to run its cold fingers through my mind. I had never gone this deep before. Water flowed into my mouth and I began to cough and sputter.

Then a firm hand took hold of my own. Strong and powerful. We moved through the water and my feet finally touched the riverbank. We had waded and swam through the current to the other side of the river. I looked back—the river was strong and powerful, for it had rained recently.

"Wow, I have never done that before." I said breathlessly.

"I can teach you how to swim. I can teach you many things." He smiled at me and I smiled back at him. I decided I liked this boy.

We crawled out of the water. It was odd how he moved; he swam like an animal. And yet he had pulled me through the current. I decided I was happy to learn from this boy. He had many things to teach me.

"My name is Ara Macao." I said proudly meeting his eyes.

His eyes danced with mirth. "Like the bird?"

"It is only common courtesy to answer my greetings and naming with that of your own," I growled at him, grinding my teeth in vexation at his foolish tongue.

"My name is Banu," he said as he took my hand as if to pull me up the riverbank.

Then he shoved me back into the mud a wide smile on his face.

I returned to my village over a month later, when my village thought me dead. My sisters I heard talk that I looked half-starved and wild, someone whispered that they saw a black panther at the edge of the woods.

After I had endured a month of hardship and came back to the village alive did the rumors of me harboring an evil spirit began.

4

In the woods we ran. The only person in the world whom I can be myself. Banu. My pace quickening, I can feel my muscles in my face relaxing as we climb to our place; a very tall tree on a hill where the spirit birds are said to roost, looking over all the living and waiting to escort them home. The rock wall prevents trespassers from gaining leverage to the heights high above. The sight of Banu ahead of me, brings on a smile. His muscles in his back ripple as he finds the hidden footholds to the secret place we go to reach the top. His hand reaches down to grab mine. A roguish grin wrecks the innocent looking face.

I know what he is up to.

"Not on my life," I say as I brush away his hand and make for the climb. He chuckles and pulls away.

"I'll beat you to the top. I always do."

"Not today! I will make it there before you!"

I hear his laughter as he begins the climb on all fours,

through the hidden pathway as I am still scaling the sheer cliff. As I said, I have an idea. I bypass the secret track up the cliff and continue to climb the perpendicular surface, my fingers strain against my weight and the ledges grow ever more dangerous. My toes are like those of a monkey or a bird, I find the smaller cracks and take hold as my fingers find the shallowest engravings to cling to.

A series of raucous caws sound the through the gully. I look up and see a pair of red parrots flying high above me, they circle before making off towards the trees but not before something hot splashes down my forehead and across my cheek. Bits of the excreta graze my lower lip.

Phaw! Disgusting!

"Of course!" I growl out as I spit. "The ancestors loath me, of course they would do this to me—"

That was when my hand slipped.

With the full weight of my body pulling against my one hand that still clung to the rock, I feel my feet slide from the cracks. I find a root that has broken through the dirt and stone and cling to it as my body gives way to gravity.

It was not enough. I fell.

And met darkness for the first time in my life.

A HEAT WARMS MY SKIN. I TRY TO STRETCH TO SOOTHE THE discomfort I feel but my shoulder pains me and I am hit with a piercing headache behind my eyes. I smell smoke and a crackle of a fire alerts me to another's presence.

I try to sit up and groan, holding my head and trying not to move my one bad arm. "Why does everything hurt?" I peek through my hand and look into the emeralds of Banu.

"Ara Macao," he begins, it comes out as a whisper on the wind. The trees shake with his words and I could feel bird flesh erupt on my skin. I love the way he says my name but... something was wrong. It was not the sound of desire—I would be a fool to think that he wanted that from me—his voice was scared. "Ara Macao." He repeated.

"Yes, that is my name," I snap at him. "Why are you so serious?"

"You don't remember?" His eyes narrow at me. Concerned. I would be touched, but that was not like him. He did not show concern or worry. He was a solid wall for me against the world. Why would he be afraid?

"What am I supposed to remember? What happened?"

"You," he says, "Fell down from the cliff."

"I fell?" Then I remember and my fingers touch my face. "Those dumb birds. They relieved themselves on me!" I sniff back my irritation. How was it that I could have been named after something so witless and foul? "They caused me to fall."

My eyes fall to Banu and there it was, the stupid smile that spreads stupidly across his face. "You looked almost cute. Like a baby in mud." Stupid answer. I could feel the heat rush to my face. He tended to do that to me with some things he would say. "But cleaned it off for you."

"You should not have touched me," I say to him, crossing my arms and wincing at the pain in my shoulder.

He moves in closer to me, I could smell his unique scent. Coal, earth and feral animal. It was intoxicating. "Let me see your arm," he says as he touches my shoulder with two of his fingers. "I am not afraid to touch you." He moves behind me and I feel his hands on my back as they slip beneath the fabric of my clothes. I am afraid he will be deterred by my filth, but he is not. His fingers slide up and down my spine, giving me fresh bumps over my body as his fingers trail down my skin. He returns to my neck and shoulder, with one hand he raises my arm gently, moving it around in circles and up and downs and in the other hand he presses and kneads the muscles of my neck and shoulder.

I sigh in relief. His fingers feel so good. I shut my eyes. With each jerk of his hand on my back, sharp pain flashes behind my eyes. But there is relief in my shoulder—or maybe healing energy from his touch that will only last with his skin on mine.

"It is not broken." His voice is in my ear, his breath tickling my neck. My arm lowers as his fingers walk up my neck.

I gasp with delight before realizing with shock at the error of my reaction. His fingers stopped their stroll. I swallow and open my eyes and turn to him. He is inches away from me. "That hurt," I lie.

He knew it. I could tell by the way he looked at me and then nods. "Let me massage your neck. I can make it feel better."

"No, don't touch me." I bite off a curse and squeeze my eyes shut with irritation at myself. "I mean, it's not my neck. It's my head. I have a headache."

"Lay down," he says to me. His eyes variegated a mix of green and oranges from the firelight. "I can help you feel comfortable."

"No," I push away from him. "I am fine, actually."

I stand to my feet and fall back down to my bottom. Banu stands and towers over me. His muscles shun in the firelight. I stared past him and then looked all around me. It had grown dark. Very dark. It was late.

"Oh no," I say, feeling anxious. "I need to go back!"

"Back, where?" He asked quietly. "You can stay with me here. You are safe with me."

"My home. I have to go back. My mama and papa will be angry. I will shame them again. The villagers already think me so wicked."

"Will they send for you? Searchers? The warriors?"

I shake my head before I could stop myself. My vision danced and swayed, and my stomach churned, threatening to upheave. I groan, letting my head fall as I shut my eyes. "I don't think they will send anyone after me. Better off dead than an annoying fly that repulses them."

He squats in front of me, his hands running through my hair gently. I don't move. I don't even breathe. "Why do you go back to them? If they hate you, stay with me. With me, you know I at least tolerate you."

The words stung. Not for the perceived insult for I took none, but for their truth in the meanings. I blink and then look at him. He smiles over at me. His white teeth shining bright. Then I shove his hand away and attempt to stand again. I did it. But barely. My world threaten to fall over again however, if I moved slowly, I could just manage to stay on my feet.

"I must go, Banu. I am sorry that I ruined our chances at a hunt." I stare off into the darkness, to the village that was somewhere in that direction. Almost, I thought I could hear my mama calling for me. Then I look back at him. He has come closer to me. I see his hand, it was reaching for me and I make to brush it away—his old tricks would not get the best of me, I think—but my arm misses his and I lurch forward and fall right into him!

Strong hands catch me and help hold me upright. He is shaking and I fear that I have upset him. "I'm all right," I tell him. He had looked so worried earlier, he must have feared for me. Then I realize he is laughing at me.

Hot white anger fills me. I raise my hand to hit him and he catches my fist in his, an arm still holds me but has fallen down to my waist. My mouth draws to a line and words begin to formulate at the end of my tongue when his lips brush against my hand.

The world freezes in time. His emerald eyes flash in the night as he catches my eyes. Then the warmth of his body warms me as he pulls me closer to him, still holding my hand in the air and my waist with the other. A smile spreads over his face. His hand releases my waist and I see it come up to my face. His hands are so warm. They caress my cheek as he stares me in the eyes. Still that smile tugs at the corner of his mouth.

He leans in close. His face less than an inch away. Cat-like eyes piercing as if seeing through me. I feel his nose brush against mine, his breath filling my mouth. The moment shatters with his silent chuckle.

"I got to go," I say to the trickster. Then I turn and run for home, my feet surprisingly steady beneath me as I flee from the forest boy. In the distance I hear a jungle cat roar.

5

One time, when I was little, I had wandered off into the woods. It was after I had returned from my month of shunning. The month of adventures with Banu. I returned on the day it would be lifted, the Shaman said if I still lived I could come home. I find my weeping mother sitting by the river's edge. I had silently waded through water too excited to see her and nervous and also, fearing what she may think. My fears were real, as I nearly scared her to death as she screamed a scream I have never heard from her before. I had not seen him, but my father was nearby, cleaning fish he had caught—only the scales as the men were not permitted to gut and bleed the kills. He barreled through the water reeds from around a rocky bank and grabbed hold of me—throwing me back into the water.

"You cannot take her soul, spirit!"

I emerge from the water, "Papa! It is me, Ara Macao!" The sun is behind him as I stand before the man who is my papa, he is dark and full of anger. I barely recognized him.

Mama's screams silence as she sees what he has done. She takes a step forward, grabbing his arm before he cuts me down with his hunting knife. "Rico, it is here! My Ara Macao has returned!"

"How can you be so certain? Look at her! She is even darker than when she has left us. Her eyes—look into them. I do not see my child. I see a wild animal." He did not lower his weapon against me. I am certain that if I raise my hand to wipe the hair from my eyes, he would have slain me.

"It is me," salty tears fall, mixing with the wetness of my hair.

"No, Rico. This is Ara Macao. Look at her."

Papa shakes his head. And then he stares at mama. No, not at mama but what she holds in her hands. She had been crying, sobbing into the red feathers of the necklace I had placed onto the riverbank. Then he looks back at me, gesturing with the knife in his hands. "Touch the charm, spirit. If you are the spirit of Ara Macao, touch it and disperse and leave my family alone. If you are my child's spirit, do this and go. Go on and do it." His knife moved left and right as he spoke.

I was too scared to move. Too scared to speak.

"You are scaring her," Mama said quietly. Tears still feel from her cheeks and she waited as if in a transfixed state. Grief filled her heart, too sad and maybe even a little fearful of feeling hope for the remnants of that had vanished after a few days of my disappearance.

"Spirits do not fear the living!" He had not taken his eyes from mine. "They pretend to be our loved ones. They cry. They beg. They trick us so they can steal our souls and take them to the void. Ara Macao was a troublesome child. Spirit—do as I say and begone!"

I sniffed back the tears. I probably looked like a demon that had just wandered out of the woods. My hair was stiff on top of my head and I had not been near a fire for so long that I was sure that I had bugs crawling in it. My nail were cracked and dirty. The rags that I had adorned around my waist had almost disintegrated. Mud and plant sap smears my skin, that I looked more a tree than a person.

I could see into my papas eyes the fear and loathing he had for me. For my troubles that I had brought to him and my people. The shame of the perceived lie. There was no love in those copper eyes. Fleetingly, the thought came to me; I could return to Banu. I would find happiness in the wilds.

The river water reaches my waist as I take a step back. It is cool against my skin. It feels nice. A temptation to return to what I had.

"Please," I hear the voice of grandmama speaking over the river's seduction. "Please, Ara Macao. Return to the living. Come home to the people." It was my grandmama. I see her, stepping through the leaves of the forest. She was here. She had seen me.

I take a step forward.

"That's right, please come home. Come to grandmama." My mama could not protect me, but I know that in the arms of grandmama that I would be fine. I would be safe. I would be loved.

My feet fly over the ground and into the arms of my grandmama. Tears flow freely as I pressed my face into her skin. Breathing in her scent. Tasting her skin against my tear stained lips as I breathed out in sobs. Her hand is in my hair and I hear soothing sounds coming from her.

"You are not to touch her!" My papa appears behind us and pulls at my hair and I am ripped from my grandmamas arms and thrown. I hold my head in agony and scream into the ground. His feet are near me and I sense danger in the air above me. "You will not take her from us!"

I look up at him, hating him as he hated me. Dark hair, lots of hair, is in the first of his hand. He sees me watching and throws it to the ground as he still holds his hunting knife. I bare my teeth and growl at him, feeling the fur on my skin rise with the tempest in my blood.

Anger is replaced by fear which is then replaced with anger once again. He sneers down at me and I feel spittle touch my cheek. I hiss up at him.

"It would see that you truly are a demon-child."

Pain explodes into my abdomen. I see papa's foot pull away from me and raise above my body readying to strike me again. The look in his eyes means death. He would kill me. My vision goes black as I begin to dwindle into unconsciousness. A panther roars its fury and I see something shoot past me, knocking papa to the ground. It stands on his chest, its long black tail flicking with righteous anger. It stares him in the eyes. Fear saturated the air.

Then it bites his face.

A battle erupts before my fading vision. Growling and screaming, not just from papa but mama and grandmama. The last thing I see is my papa running away throwing his hunting knife at the pursuing feline and missing.

• • •

***

My welcoming tonight is just like what happened in the past—it was anything but welcoming.

As soon as I am out of the forest and away from the trees, I am spotted. The village does not keep sentries, but we have hunters, the warriors, who monitor everyone. I am shocked to see them, my eyes widening as I notice Tosha's husband Caboko.

Caboko with long legs and broad shoulders—was oh so handsome. His stern stare seemed to pierce the darkness and sought me out. I approached on silent feet and even now he saw me. Though he was a few years older than Tosha and me, he was easily the tallest man in the village. Dark hair hangs handsomely down his face, grey and white feathers adorning his hair in an ornate manner fit for a man of his rank. He was an excellent hunter, the best in the village and he wore handmade adornment that Tosha had given him on their binding day; small wood and bead bracelet made from finely carved wood and holy rock. Tosha was such a showoff. If she spent her time actually helping the village, then maybe the ancestors would gift her with a child.

Caboko crossed his arms in front of me. He did not seem pleased. "So, you decided to return."

"Yeah—I fell down and just now awoke. I hurried here as soon as I could."

"You know you should not be walking in the dark. It is not good for you, Ara."

It was odd. He was not one to speak to me and his words

caught me off guard. He had addressed me with just one part of my name. As a familiar. Heat rushes into my cheeks at the implication of his words.

"I said I fell down. I was knocked out. It cannot be helped."

Concern seems to flash in Caboko's eyes. "The Spirit Talker will not be pleased." He meant the shaman. "He has made us all wear protective charms this evening. He says a shadow cat has been seen circling the village."

"Really?" I ask skeptically. The villagers always whisper that a shadow cat, a black panther, lurked in these woods around our home. I had only seen it a few times. It was always a woman who said she had seen the black cat. They were always pointing fingers at me.

He narrowed his eyes at me. "Are you saying it was not you?"

"No—it was not. I told you I fell and hit my head. I just woke."

"You sure like to sleep a lot."

I chuckle, taking his comment as a jest, few would be seen to show humor or any sort of human kindness to me. The look in his eyes said he felt affront at my laughter, that he felt mocked. I stop immediately. He really is so stern.

"I hit my head, remember?" He was stern but very dimwitted. His sign of concern had only been a lapse in judgement. I need to remember that he is not my friend. None of them are. I am an outcast.

His lips twitch as if he was on the verge of saying something. He hesitates and then shakes his head, "Get to your hut," he gestures with the toss of his head. "I will inform the spirit talker of your return. Maybe then we can be done with the charms."

"I don't know. You look good in grey and white feathers. You look like an eagle."

He narrows his eyes at me, and I fear I have just angered him. I hurry back to my little hut that was a short distance away from the shabonos. Looking over my shoulder, I saw that Caboko was gone. I think I see a bird flying over the village, grey and white, an eagle before it disappears over the hilltop.

The hut was surrounded by darkness as it sat at the outskirts of the village and was surrounded by trees and brush. I sense a presence nearby, coming from the hut. I stop and I squint my eyes, flaring out my nostrils trying to take in the scent of the unknown danger.

I could only smell the trees and the dirt of the jungle floor.

Hesitantly, I stepped forward and peered through the opening. It was dark. There was no firelight. The people of the village would not enter my dwelling without fire. Spirits feared smoke. I sighed with relief. Only Caboko had seen me and I would be in bed before the others would deign to come for me.

Briefly, I wondered about a story to tell them but then decided upon the truth. I had hit my head, and I had not been conscious until only recently. Never did it occur to me to think about Caboko. Not until I stepped through the aperture and struck the flint against the dry grass to heat the fire in the pit and saw my papa standing before me. Only then did I truly realize that the warriors had returned early and my papa was furious with me. The scar on his cheek shudders angrily.

I stepped back, dropping the flames onto the dirt floor. The fire on the grass died slowly and then extinguishes, casting the hut back into darkness just as my papa began to approach me. Fear fills me. I never try to be alone with papa. He has a temper stronger than the strongest storms. I turned and made a run for the opening and felt his firm punishing fingers on my neck as I slam to the ground, his knee between my thighs. I gasped in pain, the nights earlier trauma flashing back to the surface in white agony.

"You have disobeyed for the last time, demon child. Tonight, you receive your punishment!"

Caboko probably had not even reached the spirit walker before the entire village knew I had returned. My screams filled the night just as a panther roared its cry.

6

Voices reached my ears. I heard them long before my last scream broke my voice and only whimpers were tolerated by my vocal cords. The last thrashing ended long after the final whimpers whispered from my mouth. My body was in agony.

Oh, how I hurt.

My father left me there on the floor of my hut. Before exiting his eyes fell back to me. Tears blurred my vision as I stare back at him. There was that part of me—that willful spirit that I could never push down, as I stare into his cold dark face. His body cast into shadow as the moonlight shines from behind him.

I could never look him in the eyes. Eye contact was difficult for me. I stare at his nose, feeling the black fuzz on my shoulders and back standing on end. He returns my stare for a glare of his own. Though I cannot see his face very well, my eyes were better than most, I could sense a rictus of a sneer forming on his face as he said, "We will speak more of this in the morning."

In the woods a panther continued its roar.

Frowning my papa turned and hastily left my tent, leaving me alone.

On my arms and knees, I push myself to my bottom and hissed out in pain. "Ohhhh," I groan. My flesh protests the rough dry grass and leaves.

My ears strained to hear the voices that had carried from the fire pits around the shabonos. They were met with a stir of the wind through the forest and the growls of an animal on prowl. Fitting for one such as me, to be laying here in pain as a beast walks the woods.

"Well, come and get me." I said into dark as I crawl towards the door. It had been partially left ajar as my papa left. My head breached the threshold and I peer into the dark all around me. My hut sat at the edge of the woods—some might say it was a good distance too many past the trees. "Come on and kill me or leave me alone, spirit!" The hiss coming out of my mouth sounds more like a groan.

The forest quiets. The wind stilled. I sigh with annoyance. Pushing myself to my feet—oh how swollen and tender they felt—I began to rise, my hands pressing against the sides of the little hut, for support. The hut I call home. From here I could just see the campfire's light shining orange between the family homes where no doubt at the center the people sat around, eating fresh fruits and cooked meats. How my mouth begins to water at the aroma that drifts down towards my dwellings. I caught a little drool at the corner of my mouth and wipe at it with my hand. I am not ashamed by that. I have not eaten since the morning and that little chunk of fruit was monkey food. I craved the roast that burns on the spit. Crispy hot chunks of meat. Maybe they would have drizzled fresh fruit while the meat still cooked, giving sweet meat to the villagers.

But most of all. I want to be nearby people. Oh, how I would give anything for that. To be part of the people. A family.

I sniff back tears from the pain and the humiliation I have to suffer at the hands of my father. A man so much stronger than me. He was a warrior. A strong hunter. The men looked up to him for wisdom and virtue of strength.

Stopping the tears was like stopping a damn that had burst. They would not cease. But I was stronger than the salty water rivulets dripping down my face. I need to get to my people. I wanted to be near them. I wanted to hear the gossip and get away from the forests edge and whatever that lurked there.

I had not expected the hunters to be back so soon. It was the breeding season of some species of forest life and those creatures would travel far outside their normal ranges to find mates. Ordinarily the hunters would be gone for several days as they search for food and then made their way back.

Tomorrow I had thought. And I thought that maybe I could have brought something back before them. To show the women that I could be useful. That I am not selfish. How wrong I was.

How they dislike me.

Still. Their voices carried on the wind, the smoke of the fire and the aroma of meat drew me to them. My people.

Careful not to be caught, I make my way to the back of the shabonos where there would be fresh wood that had been cut and cut grasses to dry for weaving. From here I edged my way towards the opening where the people would be gathered. I did not need to get close. Their voices would carry with the fires smoke. I sat back, my wounds pressing against the smooth cold surface of the family hut. My father had beat me and in the pale light of the moon and the orange ambience of the fire lit torches, I could seek blue bruises forming on the back of my legs and thighs. I can only imagine how bad my back and buttocks would look like in daylight.

"What are we going to do?" One of them asks. It was Tuli. "She is out of control!"

"Someone should tell her," Tosha says with a grating edge to her voice. "She needs to be told. Maybe she will stop being so foolish if she knows the truth."

"We must do something if the traders will come back!"

Traders? What do they mean?

"She will find out when the ancestors deem it proper for her. That is how it happened to me," the voice of Aba says.

"I want my daughter to be kept safe," I hear my mama say. "Will knowing the truth help reign her in?"

"No," grandmama says fiercely. "It will only put her in danger. She is wild like the panther and hasty like a cat. The truth will only harm her."

"But if she knew—" Tosha tries again but then Okalaki breaks into the conversation.

"No, she is right, Tosha. It will only be dangerous for her if the shaman and the other men were to find out. The girl hides from us and yet she is as loud as the macaws with her complaints. She must not be told. She has to find out by herself."

"Why do we always talk about her?" Zosha chimes in. "It is

like all of our talks lately are about Ara Macao and her spirit animal. Can we just talk about something else for once?"

Though I would have agreed with Zosha, I admit, that I found this conversation intriguing. I knew they talked about me but was not present when they do. Air out the dirt. I want to know what these women truly think of me!

I sense the approach of someone coming upon the group of women and they startle when he makes his entrance. "We will find something. The people always find something to keep back the darkness and the unwanted spirits." This was the voice of the shaman. Zakopelli. The great shaman of the Ara Macao people. "She must be paired and soon." More people approach the fire, heavy footed. I can tell that the men have come after convening from their hunt. The women around the fires go quiet with their previous conversations.

I grind my teeth in annoyance.

"She is unwed," Caboko's voice chimed in in agreement with the shaman. "It is not safe for not a one of us while she is unpaired. Perhaps a paired couple can take her on and be a trio? She will be safe then; we all will be safe."

My cheeks flare anew with the presumption of me being paired with another established pair of people. It was not unheard of but not something I have considered for myself.

"And you wish to take her on, mate?" Tosha asks darkly. "You want to take on that risk?"

"Someone has to," he spoke quietly, deliberately as if thinking his words through before speaking. "I am amongst the leaders of this village. Is it not my responsibility to think about these things?"

"Let someone else open their pair up for her," Tosha growled out. "I do not agree to bringing her into our pairing."

"If not you and Caboko, then who?" Aba asks. "You two are very alike, Tosha. And I think Caboko fancies her as he fancies you. A mate of fair skin and a mate of dark skin." I could sense Aba growing heated with her words, not angry but more… excited… "I think Tonka and I need to talk." She gets up and pulls her mate with her to her family shabono.

I shift with the embarrassment. Mating was not a thing to be flummoxed over except it was me they were talking about. Me at the center of this conversation. Heat remained in my cheeks.

"A wedding then." Kali says.

Oh no. Not my sisters.

"That will be hard," Keira spoke after her sister. "She doesn't even bathe."

My face grows hot with those words. I do too bathe! Sometimes… I just forget. It's not very important when you are shunned and forgotten about. When you must hunt for food and water on your own while still having people yell at you to gather water for themselves. I am very clean. I just take hunting and gathering for myself, repairing my home so I remain dry when it rains as a little more important that swimming in the river.

"My sister mate and I cannot take her on as we are already a Trio to Bova." I hear Keira say to Kali.

"Two females is all I can handle," Bova says casually. "Sometimes too many." There were chuckles at this.

"Ohhhh, Ayyyye—" My mama moans into her hands. I peek around the corner as I draw nearer. Her own face is red with embarrassment. For herself or for me, I wonder. "My Ara Macao. What are we going to do with you?"

"Nothing mama," I whispered to myself. "Do not fret. I will hide when these people come again. Do not worry. I won't shame you." The word fell flat on my ears though I hope them to be true. I always seemed to shame my mama.

"Ohhhh, Manoa," it was the voice of my grandmama. "You worry too much about that girl and think too little of her. Give her a chance. Speak with her. All of you, you talk when you should be listening." My hero. My grandmama. "Give her a chance. She makes mistakes but who of you has ever not made a poor choice?"

"Menoakiki," It was Zakopelli the shaman. "We know how much you love Ara Macao. But you cannot deny that she runs a risk of shaming the people. With the great many deaths of the local villages, we need the traders to come to us. We need to be seen as prosperous for those who struggle right now. Our village may grow in number. Already we are felling trees to make room for more shabonos, for those peoples who have no one else because illness struck their homes. A dark spirit has walked amongst them—death has taken many lives."

"They are cursed!" Asemaki says fervently. "They have sinned against the ancestor in some way. The shadow cat has been seen in the wood and its roar is heard. We will bring the bad luck unto ourselves if we invite those wicked people into our homes."

"I agree with Asemaki," Tenki says. He is another one of the village hunters. "We will only bring bad luck and misfortune if we bring in the sinners."

"I hear you Asemaki," Zakopelli said. "I hear you, Tenki. But

I have read the holy stones, caught feathers in the air and saw which colors landed on which rocks. The tides are changing. Tomorrow or the day after, the people will be visited by the people of the water. He traders come. However, if we do not show kindness to our fellow peoples who have lost many, the stones and feathers claim that the traders will see us through water and misfortune. All of these rides on top of her being paired."

"Who will be the one to take her for mate?" The soft-spoken Pia says barely above the crackle of the fire.

"It is sad what is happening to all the other villages in the area," Okalaki says. "Is there nothing we can do for them?"

"We invite them to our peoples," the Shaman says. "But we must find Ara Macao a mate."

There was a grumble of voices. No one wanted to pair with me. Fortunately for me and for all of them, all the males had paired already. If I was to pair with any of our people, it would be with a juvenile many years my junior. It would not be good for a woman to be older than a man. It would mean the woman's spirit would be stronger than the males. And men were supposed to get spirit animals, guides for their lives. How was a man supposed to get a spirit animals respect if he was smaller than a woman's?

"Perhaps one of the survivors of the villages?" Zachi asks. She is Zosha's older sister.

"That would not be a bad idea," Okalaki says. "Get her paired and get her with babies. That will cool her spirit greatly. A mother she shall be. And then she will not run away when we women have something to tell her."

I can just see Okalaki placing her big meaty fists on her wide hips. She had born many babes that survived past their naming day and in doing so, had the body to prove her fertility. Unlike Aba, Okalaki was thick with muscles. Women looked up to her. She was the woman that arrived at a mother's side as she helps assist in the birth of their offspring.

"Then it is decided," Zakopelli says. "We will begin inviting these outsiders and hope to have Ara Macao mated before we see the face of SunFather's on the third day. For that is when the people of the waters will arrive."

"Who will tell Ara Macao the news?" Keira asks.

"Not me," Kali said.

"Ohhhh," Mama moans. "I will talk with her. I will make her see reason."

To my horror Grandmama nods as she places a comforting hand on mama's shoulder. "This will help the girl grow closer to us. She has been wild for far too long." I see her shoot father an angry stare. "And you think your hand will cool her tempest? She takes after you for her wildness. Do you disagree with her being paired?"

"No," my father said speaking up for the first time since I had snuck out to overhear what was occurring tonight. "That will not do." My father—was he speaking on my behalf? Papa? My heart churned beneath the flesh that was painful. Tears budded anew at my eyes. Hope. For the first time in a long time, I could feel hope rise in my chest. My papa. He was against what the people wanted for me. "No, it will not do to wait two full days to find her a mate and risk the disapproval of the sea people. If we are to remain tallest of the tall, we must act. To prosper, we make decisions. I say, tomorrow we find Ara Macao a mate." My father says with a dark determination in his eyes. And my heart plummets to my feet. "Tomorrow, she is to have a mate. The first man who walks into this village will have her. May the ancestors bring her a man who has a stronger will than her own."

My heart lurches.

Of course. My father would want it to be this way.

I slink away back into the darkness to where the wicked must sleep. Away from the village my lonely little huts waits for me.

7

The next day I arouse by the familiar coolness of my solitude. The world seems quiet and I realize that I am waking earlier than I normally do. I stretch and let out a groan. My body aches. I had been wary of laying on the sling last night for fear the soft fibers would be too much to bear onto my tender skin. Or too pained to crawl out from its snug embrace. Somehow, sleep came to me. My head still aches from my fall from the previous day but the pounding in my eyes is gone. I just wished the pounding in my body would follow suit.

I exit my cot, trying to squeeze through the small opening but brushing against the sides of the hut and the woven door, scraping against injuries I did not know exist until it had been made known to me.

I am immediately accosted by my sisters. Keira and Kali.

Both looked beautiful today. Keira with her hair down in dark waves, feather strewn in them. Kali, looking very much like Keira but she has her hair in a single long plait with feathers at the ends.

Despite my pains I could tell that something was not right. They were smiling at me with too large of grins, the corners of their mouth's twitching as if it pained them to do this.

"We were just coming to get you," Keira says to me. Her eyes rove over my bruised body and I could just imagine what she thought. The normal contempt for me flashed in her eyes. It was not a pretty thing to see.

"Why are you up so early? I had thought we would have to throw water on you to rouse you from the dead."

"I am up," I say to them, trying not to hold my side where father's foot had landed. "What is it you want from me?"

They look at each other. A secret they thought they hid from me passes between their eyes. "Let's go to the river," Keira says. "Perhaps you will show us your spirit animal?"

"No spirit animals," Kali says rolling her eyes. "You have foregone bathing long enough. Time to see you clean."

I glare at Keira, but my words are for Kai. "I—I don't want to be bathed right now. I hurt all over." I really did not want to see them right now, or anyone. I wanted to go to the woods, fetch my bow and my arrows and hunt with Banu. My... bow and arrows. I had brought them back with me last night. Where had I put them?

My eyes rove along the ground searching for the bow and the arrows. I had not put them back into place in the woods as I usually did. I had raced back to the village... back to... my father...

Oh no.

No. They have to be around here.

Somewhere...

Kali puffs out her cheeks, looking like a fat bird as she blew out air from her mouth. Or maybe, she looked more like a monkey about to screech in frustration. "If you stink, do you think the ancestor will heal you any quicker? You smell like the dead. Let us help you."

"I think I am fine," I say to them, peering back into my hut. Where were they? And the hunting knife? Surely I had brought them back? Caboko had stared at me funny. Yes—I had them then. He had seen them. Had he told anyone?

No. I do not think so.

It could only mean one person who could have taken them from me. My father.

"I don't think so, Ara Macao." I felt a sharp pinched right into my ribs, where all the bruising matted down my side.

"Ouch!" I exclaim and nearly tumble forward except arms grab mine and pull me towards them. "Let go of me. I don't want to hurt you. I am wicked—let go!"

"Oh Ara Macao." Keira sneered down at me. "We are not afraid to touch you, anymore."

"We know the truth about you, Ara Macao." Kali said sweetly into my ears. "The other's, and even father might fear you. But we have been watching you, ya know. You are very strange—I don't believe you are a witch or a spirit walker. I know that you are just a stupid girl who does stupid things to get attention. And you will tell us about your spirit animal."

"Poor, poor Ara Macao. The attention seeker. Yes, admit it to us here and now. It will only be good for you."

I pull my arms from their grips and they surprisingly let go

—until I hit the ground and I let out a groan of agony. My bottom is still very sore.

"You will come to the river with us Ara Macao. You will obey us in this."

"We know you are in pain. We can see the bruises. Father was lucky that he did not touch your face. It would be hard to pair an ugly face like yours with a man if it was even uglier than it is now."

"Why do you torment me so?" I ask them. I could not meet their eyes, so I looked at their noses. Their nostrils flare out like those of a tapirs. Each breath made their ears wiggle a little. I could not help but grin stupidly. It was the wrong thing to do just then.

Keira kicked me where I lay, and I folded in on myself in pain. It was not a hard kick, but it hurt.

"We do not torment you, Ara Macao. You do this to yourself. You bring shame with you wherever you go. You only think about yourself. You do these strange and unusual things to get bad attention. You behave like an animal. It is time you become a woman!"

"Be easier on her Keira," Kali says softly. "She is hurt. She won't tell us anything if you kick her. Though I wish to kick her too." She seems to remember that I am down at her feet and I flinch with the incoming kick that does not fall. "You will tell us about your spirit animal. Mothers has asked this of us. And you will listen to us. And you will be paired and mated with. It is the only way to keep you and everyone safe."

"I am not getting married!" I spat at her. "I overheard everything last night. You all squawk louder than the birds!"

"Yeah? Well I would rather sound like them than look like

their feces!" Kali says in return, her voice rising with heat. So much for speaking softly.

Vaguely, I could almost taste the squalor that had touched my face last night and I could feel myself heating with the memory.

"You cannot make me marry." I say stubbornly, pushing myself to my bottom though it pained me and then crossing my arms stubbornly.

Truthfully, I had wanted to marry, long ago. I wanted a companion. A friend. Someone I could talk to and cherish the good times with. But I did not have the good times. I did not have a friend in this village except for my grandmama. And sometimes—rarely—my mother. "I will just run away!"

"No, you won't," Keira says, folding her arms in front of her grand bosom. "You know why I think that?"

My cursed lip began to tremble as she stares down at me. I felt the words forming on my tongue before I could control myself. "Why?" I ask, stupidly.

Keira smiles. "Because you know you have nowhere to go. If you die out there in that forest, how will you go to the spirit world in the stars without the people to guide you? You would just be taken by the shadow cat."

"They say you are the shadow cats spirit walker. But that is just nonsense. You're only ugly—nothing unusual about you."

"Except she does weird things to get attention," Keira adds. "But Kali and I know that you are no spirit walker. We have seen you since birth. We were there when that man died. You were not there. In fact, we were actually with you when that happened."

"That doesn't make sense. Why would you think me not a

spirit walker and then think I have a spirit animal? You both are crazy—I—wait. What—what do you mean?"

They both smile at me. No longer the forced grin of doing their duty but true mischievous smiles. Wicked smiles.

"Don't you remember?" Kali asked me. "We were putting fruit juice on your skin and told you it would make the animal fur on your thighs and arms go away. Every time you tried to sit down—the ants would come. It was fun watching you jump up every time you sat in the grass."

Keira chuckles. "I remember that. And the surprise I felt when the people of the village came out of nowhere to collect you. You jumped up from the grass screaming and then here they come and grab you, pulling you away."

"I was a little ashamed for not saying something." Kali admits. "I thought maybe they had come to punish us. And then they took you away."

Keira shook her head at me. "You did not kill that man. And all this time you acted like you had done something wrong. You were just an annoying brat."

"Why would you not tell the others about this?" I ask them. "You have caused me a lot of sadness."

"Sadness? Was it no less than you deserved? You are always so strange, Ara Macao. It was hard to have sympathy for you."

"And you continually shame us all," Keira says. "But now that is ending. You know the truth. You are not special. You are not a wicked spirit walker. You are just a brat seeking attention from your betters."

Tears stung my eyes and I shamefully wipe them away. "I cannot believe this of you two."

"Well—believe it." Kali says. "It's the only time we will ever speak of it."

"You're not going to tell the others? Tell them what you have done?"

"We have done nothing, Ara Macao." Keira sneers. "We have always been good women. Good wives. Our children are good kids. We help out around the village and the people respect us. You on the other hand have done nothing to garner favor."

"No one will believe you if you say anything, Ara Macao," Kali says. "We only tell you this truth, so you know you are no different from anybody else. Just uglier. And now, it is your time to fulfill your duty as a woman."

"Grandmama says you have the makings to be a spirit walkers."

"The next female shaman," Kali agree.

Keira and Kali reach down, both taking one of my arms and pulled me to my feet. They let go as if they expect me not to run away. Not to want to punch neither of them. My hands ball into fists at my sides.

They are right.

How could I raise my hand to either of them? If what they said is true, then I am not different from them. Just darker skinned and hairier. But that left my eyes…

And they still think I have a spirit animal…

And grandmama says that I could be a spirit walker and the next female shaman? Lies. Blatant lies. Grandmama would never say such a thing about me.

"My eyes are different that yours," I say thoughtfully as I looked into their dark brown. I can't help but feel that there was something there about that, something that halted my anger with realization.

Kali sniffed and Keira's mouth thins into a line. "It is the only thing pretty about you. The only thing that will attract a man's attention."

They are jealous of me.

They. Are. Jealous. Of. Me.

8

The sky is still dark, but I feel the first signs of SunFather coming to warm the earth. There are clouds in the sky, normal for this time of year and this unholy time in the day. Mornings were never comfortable—worse than night as one could sleep through the chill that sometimes came when MoonMother was in the sky. The sound of the river churned with its effortless current. The water spirits were active already.

"Bend your head down—you are too tall for me to do this comfortably."

I bend my head obliging my sisters, although I was already kneeling onto the riverbank, my knees deep in the mud. Soft sweet-smelling grasses have been crushed together with even sweeter scenting plants—sickly sweet that I feared that they were rubbing poison into my strands of thick hair. Then they apply the mud. Caking it on top of the drying plants. It feels wet and cold and good against my scalp.

"Stop moving," Kali complains. "You will never be clean if you move away."

"You're being too rough," I say bitterly.

"Ara Macao, you say that as if we enjoy doing this." That was from Keira who scrubs my skin with small river rocks and the softer muck that was on the bottom of the moving water.

"Don't you? My tormenters…"

"That again? You sure are repetitive. As long as you do not start passing a feather between your fingers or rolling a rock over your knuckles."

"That is so embarrassing. Please do not do that."

Now that they mention it, that sounds exactly what I want to do. With my head lowered I scour the ground for a perfect little pebble. It could not be imperfect for that would not be correct. I need to be round, smooth and white. White against my dark skin so I could see the little rock move. All I see are little brown and black misshapen pebbles.

"Oh no—she is looking for a rock." Kali tugs on my hair. "Stop it, Ara Macao. You need to stop that strangeness."

"Next thing we will see is her counting or explaining strange things that only she could see."

I blink my eyes and my hand stills in their search for the perfect rock. Were they planting these ideas in my head? I glance up at them and they broke into fits of laughter.

"Next she will spin around a tree saying she has to untangle herself!"

More laughter.

Despite the cool water of the river, I could feel myself heat up with embarrassment. My sisters always make me feel so self-conscious in all of my actions. They claim that these things that

I did were not normal. That I do things for attention. But I could not help it. They were my little quirks. Quirks that I could not resist. The temptations agonize me more than the bruises on my body.

And I feel angry at myself for wanting to give into these impulses.

"Ara Macao, it is time you listened to us on how to become a woman." Keira says behind me. She begins to drone on about womanhood and preparations of mating. I ignore all of it.

From the other side of the riverbank, the green eyes of a black panther stared back at me. For some strange reason, the thought of Banu entered my mind. I blink and the shadow cat is gone.

MY HAIR HANGS IN MANY LOOSE BRAIDS WITH FEATHERS adorning the plaits. I smell of fruit, blossoms and river water but more importantly I no longer smell like the bottom of a foot. My skin was clean. My face and hair did not itch, and I could run my fingers through my hair—prior to the loose braids I could not move my hands through my hair.

The young children dance around the fire, playing in their youth. Girls throwing wet grasses and dried flowers and special herbs into the blaze to creature smoke and sweet scents. The boys would take sticks and poke at the flames, shoving and pushing each other for the better spot.

The first of the travelers began to come into our village today. Groups of women with children. Grandparents and some young. The women in my village accepted them with open arms, taking the children to play with the kids of our village and embracing the women both young and old as though long, lost friends. It had been so long since our people had traded with another villages.

Illness had wrecked the land again with the spotting of the shadow cat. People were dying. Entire villages were abandoned in the forest when the hunters failed to return from their exploits. Women left to tend to the sick until there was nobody left but them and whoever survived.

Not a single young man had come seeking refuge or to call our village home. Only women and the old. There were a few older men who had lost their minds to the withering of age. They sat with the children and the kids played on top of them. Grandmothers sat nearby, talking to the elderly women of our village.

In a single day our village has doubled in size.

As SunFather rose in the sky and MotherMoon disappears into the treetops, another Shabono had been erected in the clearing. The hunters of our village strived to create shelter before the new arrivals would come. Weeks ago, the Shaman had suggested the hunters to strip bark and split wood, dry grass and make thatch for there would come a time when more Shabonos would be required.

I sit in the warmth of the sun, center of the women in the village. They saw my clean skin, my braided hair and feathers that had been adorned and knew that I was seeking a mate. I am not very hopeful.

Begrudgingly, I relish being part of something.

My jealous sisters are wrong. I do not seek attention, nor do I bask in it. But I will admit that I enjoy being part of the people. Being part of something important—even if it is something that I do not support. I do not wish to be marry. To pair up and mate. I do not want children. I do not want to be tied down by womanly desires. I want to be free. To be me. To be with Banu in the forest. That is where I was am comfortable. Maybe long ago I would have liked all of this, but it is not me.

Even despite my despairing feelings of the idea of pairing, I relish being in the center of all the happiness. Happiness at the prospect of a pairing happening. A new couple mating was always a time for rejoice.

"Ara Macao," my mama says sitting by my side. She pulled something from her back and the women nearby stop doing what they are doing and ohhhh'd and ahhhh'd. Making big eyes and gestures of appreciation. Mama pays no mind to their flattering attempts and hands me the cobija; it was made of fresh white flowers, entwined with feathers of every color. This was a gift from a mother to her daughter before she took a man for a mate.

I blush at the symbol that it represents. Sexuality. Fertility. I looked around and do not see any strange men coming into the village. A couple of the women near me chuckle and I could not help but smile shyly.

"Ayyyye-e-e—Ara Macao! You are far too dark to be sitting out in the sun like this. You will only get darker." Now this did cause laughter from those who overhear my mama. "This isn't supposed to be worn until the man takes you to his tent. But I do not want you to scare a man away. Look at you, your skin is covered with black fur. This will not do. You must push back the spirit animals attempts to hold you to him." I look up at her sharply for she whispers the last to me as she brushes away some of my braids from my ear. "You can tell me about him. Let me help you, my child."

That is when I notice Keira and Kali standing a short distance away. They did not look pleased.

"What is it?" I ask. Feeling nervous beneath all these eyes. All this unwanted attention.

"We need to help you remove the fur on your arms and back of your neck. You cannot show a man you are an animal. He will not have you looking how you do."

"What?" I sputter, feeling heat rise to my cheeks in full force as more laughter erupted from all these strangers. I am so glad that he village men were convening away from us right now—always doing men things with the village leader, my fathers and the shaman. But it still hurts to be the center of these new people who wish to mock me for my differences.

When I learned that our village might be getting misplaced people from other villages there was a part of me that had grown hopefully.

With new people in the village, I had hoped, that maybe… maybe they would see me as a person and come to respect me by my actions. I had hoped, that they would not immediately dislike me. I could see now that I might have been wrong to have hoped.

What was I thinking?

I snatch a couple rocks in my hand on the ground—out of the three pebbles one was white—and I began to roll the little round stone between my fingers and over my knuckles.

"Stop that strangeness, Ara Macao," my mama says, snatching at my hand.

My eyes go wide as I realize that mama has just touched my

hand. Her hand rests on mine and I am in shock and don't move away from the feeling of her hand on top of mine.

"What is she doing?" Another woman asks.

I bit my lip, hoping that my mother will keep my secret my own.

"Rolling a rock between her fingers. Ayyyye-e-e. She is a strange one."

"Too dark. Too much sun cooked her brain," the woman says with a sympathetic smile on her face.

"Ayyyye-e-e. That happens when you do not protect yourself and stay in the sun for too long."

"Poor girl," another one says. "This is probably the reason she is being paired so late in her life. She must be almost sixteen."

"Her eyes are a strange color."

"Does she have a… you know?"

The voices. They were coming from everywhere. The voices of damnation. The eyes, the looks. I squeeze my eyes shut and put my hands over my head and felt myself rock. This brought on more words of persecution. My heart begins to beat hard in my chest.

A firm hand landed on my shoulder, squeezing hard. I gasped out in pain—my body was still so sore, and it had taken a while to find a place of comfort on the dried grasses. I look through my arms and up into the face of my father. Gone was the papa I had always seen him as. This was a man who I did not recognize. A man who looks willing to hurt me again.

"Enough with your strangeness, girl. You are shaming us."

I stare at him; long and hard and feeling anger and hatred begin to fill my heart. Then I realize that everyone is looking at us. No… not us. Me. They are staring at me. Even the children by the fire have stopped their play to look at me with suspicion. They are all against me. I could not start over with new people. They were all the same. Those eyes—the eyes of judgement.

I smack his hand from my body and a look of rage marred his features before they cool into discontent. I rose to my feet on weak wobbly legs—they were still sore from the thrashing this man had given me not even twenty-four hours ago. I saw both of my sisters start forward before they stop, hesitant. What could they be thinking? They didn't want to get in between the man they love and the sister they hate?

"Maybe you should stop asking me to stop when it is you who should stop shaming yourself. All of you! Damn you all!"

I flee the gathering.

Arms try to catch me as I ran past. I see Keira and Kali reach for me, but they only succeed in pulling the cobija from my shoulders as I ran bare skinned into the forest. Shouts follow me as I continue to run, continue to flee from their eyes of judgement.

9

____

The river passes before me in its continuous never ending current. Some months of the year the current would be hundreds of people wide, and other times of the year only twenty people wide. Some years were worse than others but always the river will always be. The noise of the river sometimes helps comfort me when I am angered. The churning current and an occasional splash of fish and other underwater creature alerted me to their presence. It was unsurprising when a snap of a twig behind me alerts me of another presence.

It is not Banu.

His feet are silent. He walks on the balls of his feet, such quiet feet that seem to absorb any noise he makes. That boy could jump and crash to the ground and there would barely be a hush of wind.

I turn and was surprised at who I see approaching me. It is my grandmama.

Though I should not be surprised. Before Banu, she has

been the only friend I have ever known. She is so like my mama but kinder, more compassionate and genuinely seems to care for me.

Except my sisters say that grandmama thought me a spirit walker… a female shaman…

I wipe my eyes—shame eats at me; the tears seem to come too easily—and I stand to greet her. If she had been my mother approaching me, I would have jumped into the river and faced the caiman in the waters, something I would never do unless Banu was around. His presence seemed to keep the big water reptiles away.

"I'm sorry grandmama," I whisper as she nears. "I do not mean to shame you. If I had a choice, I would never bring you shame. I'm sorry grandmama." I could not control the tremble to my lip. Why did I feel so powerless right now? My emotions seem to be getting away from me lately.

"It is all right, child." Grandmama steps to my side and then does something that surprises me. She sits where I had been siting a moment before, right into the river reeds and plants, sticking her toes into the moving water. "I know you like to fish. Maybe I just might catch something for you and me to eat?" She wiggles her toes just below the surface of the water in a dramatic display that I couldn't help but laugh with her.

I sit by her side and stick my own feet into the water. "More feet will help lure them to us."

"Very good child," she says. "When they get near, I'll continue to wiggle my toes and you make a grab for one."

"Sounds like a great plan, grandmama." I hiccup. My grandmama looks over at me and put an arm over my shoulder. Then she leans her head against mine.

"Will you keep a secret?" She asks me. Her voice growing seriously.

I try to turn and look at her, but her head is squishing against mine, and I could not look at her nose to see if she was jesting. I try to speak but my voice catches in my throat, so I nod my head but only half succeed at that. Yet my grandmama sensed that I answer with my movement and didn't need to wait to hear me speak before she replies, "This secret I only tell you. And I trust you to keep it to yourself."

I nod my head again, feeling her soft cheek still firmly against my own. She smells like a baby bird. A sharp, unusual scent. Her own scent.

"You are my favorite grandchild," she says seriously. "Don't tell your mama, or papa."

"You forgot to tell me not to mention it to Kali and Keira. They admit that my eyes were pretty earlier. I think they have been jealous of me for so very long, though I know not why. How can they call me ugly and yet believe my eyes are beautiful?"

"That is because you are not ugly, child. You are just different. We are all different." Grandmama sighs and then turns and looks at me. Our noses were just inches apart and this close I could see that her eyes were beginning to cloud. "You are my favorite and you can tell that to your sisters. Just not your parents."

I chuckle uncomfortably. "That will not go well. They are no longer afraid of me."

Grandmama turns to stare at the water. "Then they are fools."

I turned, feeling shock and then look at my fingers in my

lap. My eyes land on the bruises on my arms, then at my thighs and torso. I'm all bruises. "I don't think they are the fool."

"No, they are fools. Being split at birth can do that to a soul."

"Grandmama," I say forcefully. "They are no longer afraid of me because they know I am not special. That I am not different —except for my looks. I am human. I am not a spirit walker. And I think they are right."

"You do?"

"Yes," I say, nodding my head, finding that my voice came on more strongly now. "All of my life I thought I was wicked. That I was something of evil origin. Now I know I am wrong. Look at me, grandmama. I am covered in bruises. For years father has beat me. For years everyone has known of it but has said nothing but horrible things to me. It was to keep me controlled because… because… because I am strange. I have these weird quirks about myself that I cannot stop even if I wanted to. Because I look different. Because my eyes glow green. I…" my throat began to seize up, and fails me again, and I stare into the grass, searching for a rock to twirl between my fingers, or a sharp blade of grass to poke between my nail and my fingertip.

"They think you think that I am a spirit walker and that I have a spirit animal. I think they are wrong. I do not think you think these horrible things of me. Look at me grandmama, you know me."

"What about the shadow cat that follows you everywhere you go?" Grandmama asks.

My head snaps up. "Shadow cat?"

"Yes, child. I know of it."

"I have only just seen it. It is the death of the other villages. It is a sign. An ill omen. It's—"

"No, child. It is your spirit animal."

"No grandmama. I am normal. I am not special."

"Why do you say that?" Grandmama looks at me, a perplexed look in her cloudy eyes.

"Because father beats me. My sisters touched me. Yet they are not dead. Nothing bad had happened to them. It was all a lie, grandmama. Don't you see?"

"No, child. I don't see very well anymore. But I do listen. And what I don't hear people saying is words enough. And—there is the account of the strange black panther that trails you wherever you go. You cannot deny it."

"I—"

"When your father hits you, a panther can be heard roaring in the trees."

"I—"

"When you run in the woods, the hunters find panther tracks following you and yet you always return unharmed."

"But if they knew it hunted me, wouldn't they have killed it?"

"Not a black panther. To kill one such as it means death to all. For a long time, the people have hoped that the panther would take you away—yet you return after every escapade. It angers your father because it makes him be weak before the men in the village. His spirit animal is the jaguar. A strong and noble warrior. A symbol of strength, it is why he is such a brave and powerful hunter. And you have a panther as a spirit animal when the men believe that women cannot have spirit animals. And yours is the black panther. A powerful spirit. You have the makings for a female shaman. You are the last spirit walker of our village."

I sigh and look into the water. My sisters are right. Grandmama did think that I was a monster.

"Grandmama, how could you say these things?" The question hurts to come out and I say it as gently as I can. I love my grandmama but to hear her say these things about me hurt me. I could be honest with her; I can be myself with her. "It hurts me to think you think these things about me."

"Sometimes the truth is not something we want to hear."

"You do believe that I am a spirit walker then?" I choke back the sob threatening to come. "You believe I have this spirit animal?"

Grandma sighs. "You need to be told something, child. The things you believe are not true. Not the full truth. Please let me tell you something about yourself, your people, your village."

A blur dashed in front of my eyes beneath the water. A fish was coming towards our feet. Grandmama had not relented in her wiggling toes despite the long talk. I decide to up my game and try to lure it to my big toe before hers. She looks at me and a grin broke out on her weathering face.

Game on.

"You are special, child. More special than you realize."

"I don't understand, Grandmama. I don't feel special. But you think I am a spirit walker..."

"You are bonded to a spirit animal—if not bonded, then you are well on your way to bonding one. It will not allow you to find a mate, child. Know this, it will prevent you at all cost. Do not break its trust. A spirit animal is a being you need more than a mate. They are protectors."

"I—I don't need a protector."

"No, child, you do We all do."

"I don't want it!" I wiggle my toes harder as if that will attract the fish.

Grandmama hesitates before replying. "Then you can kill it. Though I think you need to speak with more women of the village. To understand what you do not understand. I do not suggest doing this evil thing. Killing a spirit animal, no matter what sort of animal, is evil."

"Kill?" I ask and immediately grow wary. I had only seen this cat a few times in my entire life. Did I want to kill something I could never see? I look back into the woods, lush green jungle looks back at me. How could I kill something that stalks so effortlessly? Briefly, I hope that Banu was safe in the woods. He too, lives in this forest. "I do not think I wish to kill it. It has not harmed me or the forest boy. I don't want a spirit animal and will not kill it."

"No child, you misunderstand," Grandmama says, shaking her head. "You are already bonded to it, or close enough. It is attracted to you now. To kill it is to break that bond and in return break something of yourself because it is who you are."

"Oh," I say, feeling foolish. "I have only seen this spirit walker a couple of times."

Grandmama's face scrunched up as she grew thoughtful. Then with a surge of energy her foot came flying out of the water with a large fish attached—not to her toe but on her foot!

I jump up, pulling my feet from the water and make a grab for the fish—when I see a shadow in the water staring back at me. A black large shadow. With green eyes reflecting back at me before I fell headfirst into the water.

10

Water enters my mouth and fills my lungs. I try to cough and spit it out but that only brings in more. My bottom hits the river bottom as I try to kick up off the ground and I realize that my body has grown sluggish and slows. Worry fills me as the corners of my vision begins to turn dark—which is not from being submerged in the murk of the water. I try to break to the surface, but feel my forehead graze the top before I sink with the underwater current pulling at my feet.

I am drowning!

How stupid am I? I, a person who lives on the river and the forest. I, who swim with the weird Banu and out swam crocodilians and the lurking giant snakes. I…am… drowning.

My arms feel stiff, my legs twitch aimlessly, futile. I could feel my body put forth the last struggle to live. I am dying. As my vision begins to go dark, I hear a splash and then strong arms wrap around me.

Wind hits my head as I break free from the water. Vaguely, I see a dead fish on the shore. My grandmama was nowhere to be seen. Probably had ran to get help when I had fallen into the river.

My chest feels full on the point of bursting and as I stare at the bright blue sky, I fall into darkness.

Something jumps on my chest. Once. Twice. Three times. And water trickles up from my lungs. It is not enough. Again, the pressure on my chest. Something, no, someone is hitting me. Pounding into me. Then a rough touch to my face as whoever it is tries to blow the life of air into me. I lay there, paralyzed on the border of unconsciousness and death.

Suddenly as if through an underwater current traveling through me, the water spews from my mouth and nose and I vomit everything I have ever eaten in my life. And then I do it again. The entire river roared in my ears and spills out in front of me.

Automatically, my lungs sucks in its first agonizingly sweet breath of air, my back arching with the process before falling down onto my size, coughing and hacking as if I have breathed in bad smoke. I lay there for a very long time between fits of coughing and sucking in air. The sound that comes to my ears is odd. Wheezing, wet, nasally.

The world passes me slowly as I regain my breath.

I roll onto my back. And Banu stares down at me. His green eyes—eyes like my own—looked worried until he sees me staring back at him. Then he smiles. Oh, how I love that smile.

"Banu—" I try to say before a coughing fit overtook me. He waits patiently at my side, a hand resting on my hips. "You saved me?"

"If you are making a habit of this," he says coquettishly. "I will need to make sure I am always around for when you decide to play these games with me."

I try to push him away teasingly, but it came as a flopping hand. Or a dead eel. I couldn't decide which, but the thought makes me laugh. His smile grew larger as he stared down at me and I laughed harder.

"Where did you come from?" I asked him. "I was alone here with my grandmama when I saw—that's right. I saw a panther in the water. I thought it had come for me. Banu—you must take care! There is a spirit walker in these woods—and they say it's me!"

He frowns down at me, his face is the image of concern.

"My grandmama confirmed it for me. Ohhhh, Ayyyye-e-e! I hope she did not run into it as she ran to the village."

"I don't think you have to worry about that, Ara Macao. It is not here. Just you and I." His hand was very hot on my skin. My legs were parted, and I felt the wind kiss my wet skin with its cold breath.

And that is when I realize I was naked.

For my people and most of the forest peoples, we do not mind our skin. It was not shameful or embarrassing to be seen in our skin. We did take delight in clothes, especially in the downy soft materials that the traders used to bring us. But we did not feel like we had to wear anything. The very little children went naked. Half the women of childbearing age were bear to SunFather from their waist up, though some cover when they are no longer with a babe that nurses. The men wore materials made of animal hide around their loins but even then it was not necessary. The very old often wear nothing.

I am naked as the day I was born.

Banu has always worn the cloth at his loins. Now, he, too, is naked. His skin glossy black in SunFather's light. Water still trails down from his matted hair, down his chest and limbs.

His hand is firm and strong on my hip. His nails clean. His skin as kissed by SunFather as my own. And he does not seem to mind.

In fact—he did not seem to care at all. From the heat radiating from his body and the growing manhood, he is pleased.

"Banu, I—"

His fingers trailed up from my waist, snaking up the feminine curves of my body and to my left breast. "I thought I lost you."

"Banu…"

I lay very still; my skin seems to instantly dry and form bird-skin around his hot hands. Gently, he caresses my bosom, his fingers tugging wickedly at my nipple.

"Oh, Banu." I try to sit up, but his playful hand suddenly became firm on my chest until I lay back down.

"Be still," he said, seriously. "Let me be sure that you are ok." A roguish grin threatens to tug at his mouth, but he controls it and kept the seriously look on his face. "That is if it is all right with you."

"Alright with you?"

"To touch you. To show how much you mean to me." He slid past the left breast and snaked his fingers across my collarbone and my neck, poking at the bruises and then shooting to the right nipple.

I chuckle and grab at his hand. He instantly stills and begins to pull away. "No," I whisper. "I nearly just died. Please, don't stop. I want to feel you. If this is a dream that I will wake from, please don't stop now."

That roguish smile spreads across his face. "You want to feel me?"

"Yes," I say.

"Where?" he asks.

"Everywhere," I tell him. He circles my breast with his middle fingers before running his hands down my stomach again and to my thighs.

"Here too?"

I nod my head.

I tried to shut my legs from the wind, but his firm hand pried them apart and he gave me a disapproving look. Slowly, with both hands, he began to massage my upper thighs and down to the knees, all while keeping my legs slightly apart. Then… his warm fingers dip and begins to knead at the muscles of my inner thighs. And made their way back up to—

I gasp with shock and delight. His fingers were not probing but they touched my sex gently, experimentally palpitating and using two fingers to gently touch my lips down between my legs. The middle finger tapped my sex.

I moan with pleasure, and pull my knees up, exposing myself to his deliberations. He smiles as he begins to palpate my sex in a rhythmic beat before he brought his other hand up to explore the lower area of my pleasure.

This was not the first time we have messed around and I hoped it was not the last. I may not have his roguish heart as my own for he was the forest boy and I the village outcast, but for now, we had each other's bodies for comfort.

11

I lay there, sprawling out in the grass as my fingers play with the tufts of baby river weeds. SunFather's warmth heats the ground and bakes my skin as I am feeling content. Banu, lays in front of me, he is on his side and though he faces me, his eyes roam the river the riverbank before they return to me. He smiles. This time it is a gentle touch on his lips.

"Banu, I—"

"Ara Macao?" he whispers, and I blush under his intense stare.

He had touched me. Gently at first before working up to a passionate lather. Yet—he did not get his own pleasure for it. He had done it for mine. I blush furiously. Usually we mated enjoy panting animals, but this time he had done it just for me.

I wished that he would have come from a village for it would mean that he and I could be paired. But he was a forest boy… an outcast beyond the ranking of my own outcast for I still had a village to call home.

"Ara Macao," he says again. "You wish to ask me something?"

"I…" Rolling onto my back, I rub at my eyes. My body still feels sore, but the muscles now feel more relaxed than they have ever been. I stare up at the blue sky. "Banu," I begin again. "How—how did you become a forest boy? What happened to you? I fear that whatever you did, I am doing, and I will become a forest girl, too."

He lays there, quiet. I look over at him and he has a pensive look shadowing his face. "I was just born different, like you. But unlike you, I have always been alone."

"Really? But there must have been a time you remember your family? Which village did you come from?" I cannot believe that I have never asked him these questions. I have always accepted him at point blank and I still do, but now that I had thought of the question, the words are out in the open, and so I wonder.

He sighs. Then rolls to his stomach, his pectoral muscle flexing with the movement. He does not see me biting my lip as he sniffs at a water lily very much like a cat.

I giggle.

He looks over at me and smiles. "I cannot remember any of that. I have always been alone."

"What is your first memory? Maybe going off that we can have a general geographical location of where you originated from?"

"I remember seeing you."

"You what?"

"At the edge of the woods, crying. You looked so small. So young. Maybe it was your tears that had attracted my attention, or the way you stared at me as I approached you.

You were not afraid of me. You reached out your hand and touched my face."

"I don't remember this. When was this?"

He looked over at me and frowned. "It was before you came to the woods, banished from your village for an entire moon cycle. You saw me in the woods. Talked to me. Then you told your people I was in the forest. Those are my earliest memories."

"That cannot be. You must have been six or seven. Little older than myself."

He shrugs, his nose pressing into the flower. "But it is true. I don't have any earlier memory than you."

"Your earliest memory is of me?" I whisper the words. But how could that be? Then I swat at his arm, he turns frowning at me. "You have a bad memory, Banu. If my ugly face is the earliest thing you can recall, you are hopeless. I know babies who remember things."

"Your face isn't ugly, Ara Macao." His face is all serious now as he sits up. "If fact, it is the most beautiful one I have ever seen."

"You just say that. You haven't seen the women in my village. Even some newcomers are prettier than me. Well—probably not some, but all of them. You have to see them. Beautiful women and not all of them are paired."

"I don't want to," He says, folding his arms. "I don't care for anyone in that village of yours's. You are the prettiest girl I have ever laid my eyes upon."

"Ayyyye-e-e," I groan. "You tempt me with your vile sweet talk. I know the truth though."

"Are you sure about that, Ara Macao? Because all the things

you have just said are lies in my ears. You are the gem hidden in the water, while they are the plain river rock along the banks."

My heart flutters. I blink with surprise at myself more than him. His words touches something inside of me. Nobody has ever spoken to me like that. Ugly. Hairy. Strange. Those are the words that describe me. Yet, this boy, Banu, he claims otherwise.

"Beautiful, eh?" I say sarcastically. "You are the first to say so." I roll to my stomach and stare at my fingers. A rock plays between them, rolling on top of my knuckles to the tips of my fingers before coming to my palm and back over my knuckles. My odd quirks. Today a rock. Tomorrow a tree branch. The next day, I'll be squeezing myself through small openings, between logs, and swerving through the foot trails of grass, being sure not to touch anything that has not already been walked on. "If you told me that I am strange, I'd believe you. Mention the hair on my body, I would nod at your words. If you called me ugly, I'd trust your judgement. But beautiful? Well—you flatter well."

"It is true." He nods at my words and I smile in relief. He was seeing reason. "You are beautifully hairy."

I glare at him and threaten to smack him again, but he chuckles and flicks the little flower in front of him. "I don't want you to pair bond with another man, Ara Macao. The thought makes me want to go crazy."

"You what?" I turn to him, frowning at the change of topic.

"I don't want you to pair with a random man that has come into your village."

"How do you know about this?"

"I hear things in the woods. The peoples are loud, and I listen."

"Not only do you flatter, you stalk me. If I am strange, then I have learned it from the master. You."

"Probably," he says but his jaw is serious. "But that doesn't change the fact that I don't want you to be with another man. I don't know if I can control myself if that happens. The mere thought makes me very angry."

I sigh. "But you know that I have to pair. It has been decided. My father and the people will be shamed if I don't. It is bad luck to have an unpaired woman while the traders come. It brings on lust from the strange men of the sea. Some say that is why Tosha is so pale because her mother was taken by one of the tradesmen, though Toshin will not admit it. The shaman said that they come in two days. In two days, the tradesmen will arrive. I have two days to have seed spilled in me and be claimed."

"I can do that," Banu says breathlessly. "I will claim you."

"Banu," I say sadly as my groin gives a twinge at the prospect. "What we do on the river is play. Bestowing seed is claiming. I have never let it get that far. You spill it on the flowers you so casually sniff."

"Yeah, I understand all of that." He doesn't bat an eye at the flower he is poking at.

"And you will claim me?"

"You spend a lot of time with me already. Are you not already mine?"

I laugh and then a smile breaks on his face. "If only it were so simple."

"It is," he turns serious again. "Stay with me."

"What is your meaning?" I fear what he might say. These words were walking a fine line of sin. I could not stay with a forest boy. A boy… no… a man, for that is what Banu is and a man without a people. Who would guide him to the ancestors when he died? And if I were to live with him in the forest, who would guide my spirit?

A spirit animals is claimed to be in these woods, and it has been haunting me most of my life. If I lived in these woods, I would be inviting death and the spirit walk to claim my soul.

"Stay with me in the forest. Be mine."

I sit up, rubbing my arms of their little cold bumps. His words run along a hope I have always wanted but knew could not be. He was a forest boy, and I still had a people who were mine. "Me, stay with a forest boy? Become a forest girl? I—I don't know Banu. I enjoy being with the people. I want a family… I think. And most of all, what about my soul when I die? What about yours? I think that is why I like you. I enjoy your free spirit but what will happen when you are called back to the stars?"

"Then stay with me for the next two days!"

"Two days?" I ask, stupidly. I wanted an eternity with this man. If only it could be.

"If you do not return, you need not pair bond with another man."

"But that is the point. To become pair bonded and claimed. So, my soul can be tied down to the peoples and my spirit guided back to the ancestor in death."

He shakes his head in disbelief. "I cannot believe that you believe in such a thing."

"Do you not believe it so?" I ask, testily. "We may look

different from the people, but we are the same as them. We have the ancestors who are the people we return to in death if we are guided back. If we do not have a guide, then the spirit walker will claim us." He looks back at me, shaking head. "If you die, Banu. I will find your body and light a pyre and put the right flowers and feathers, so that you will fly home."

"Are you saying you want to be with another?" He asks darkly. "That you want to be pair bonded and mated with another?"

I sigh, feeling confusion. "I don't know." I pull my legs up to my chin and stare into the water. After some time, I hear Banu sit by my side. Then felt his body against mine. He is hot, his warmth flooding into me. It is intoxicating.

"Do you hear that?" He asks.

I stare at him. "Hear what?" I strain my ears, trying to catch the subtle sounds of the forest and hear nothing.

"Nothing. No cries of alarm. No running feet. We have been on this bank for some time. Yet—no one has come to try to fish you from the river. You would be dead."

"I—"

"I don't know what I will do if you are pair bonded. If you go back right now. I don't trust myself."

"What do you mean?"

"I won't allow another man to set foot in that village while you are to be mated. The first man, your father said. The first man to walk into your village will have you. And I won't allow that."

"Are what are you going to do? Stop them."

"I might," he growls.

I look down at my hands, spinning a tuft of baby reeds

between my fingers. "My father will be very angry if I do not return."

"For all your father knows, you are dead. They all think that. I am the only one that cares for you." I open my mouth and he glares at me to make me silent. "Look at your poor body, Ara Macao. Look at how that vile man has hurt you. I heard you crying out. It took all of my will to not rush into your village to hurt your father. To hurt everyone who allowed that to happen to you. No one cares for you at that village. I care for you, only me."

He was right, of course. No one had come to the river. There had been no cry of alarm or search party to find me. Except… there was one other person. "My grandmama would not have left me to drown."

"You are right," he said. "But do you think they would have allowed her to try to come back for you? To possibly drown in the river alongside you. No, they would not. Your grandmama is full of wisdom and respect."

"Whereas I am not?"

He looks at me and didn't say a word. He didn't need to. I knew the truth.

"Why would I return after two days, then?"

"Because you want to? And I want you to do what makes you happy."

"You make me happy," I say, shyly.

Banu smiles at that. "Yes, but you also need your people. I don't understand it. They do not treat you well and I hate that. I hate them. But you… you love them. I have to respect your feelings on this. I would love for you to stay in the forest with me, forever but respect your feelings on returning despite it being foolish."

"But you won't respect my feelings on finding a man to pair bond and mate with?"

He seemed to tense up, confusion and full of passion. "No, I don't think so." He crosses his arms and looking petulant.

I sigh again and stare at my toes, wiggling their way into the soft river mud. "I will be beaten if I return now after they presumed me dead in the river. My father will want to prove that he has power over me and that I am not dangerous. I don't want to be beaten again. I hurt. And if I don't return now and wait two days…"

Banu seems to grow even more tense, as if sensing my answer in the air. What did he want to hear from me?

"If I don't return now and wait two days… I will still be beaten."

If I do not return now and wait, I will be unmated and unpaired, but Banu will be happy and ultimately, so will I. I did not want to pair up with anyone my father says who walks into the village. I would be free, forever free and with Banu. Even if I could not have him in truth, I can have him in this. As a friend. When I returned, the village would not be able to pair me up for the traders will have come and my father's words would fall on deaf ears. I will prove to him that me being unpaired will not ruin our village's chance at a trade. I will prove to them all that I was not someone to bully and that my presence was not evil.

He frowns at me but did not say anything, letting me decide this monumental moment. I suddenly rise to my feet and in doing so, Banu follows my action. A little V formed between his eyes brows as he looks at me, worried.

I smile at him. "I will need to make another bow and sling of arrows."

He grins and holds out his hand to me. "I have one of your hunting knives, still. It will have to do."

And I took his hand. For the first time in my life, he did not push me away in a trick, instead we run, hand in hand, into the woods.

12

I crouch, waiting. Something or rather, someone, is out there.

It has been almost two days since I have roamed the forest with the forest boy, Banu. He gave me the hunting knife; he was very adept at catching and cornering game—whereas I needed something in my hands. I also, believe, that he felt that I needed far more protection than he did. He knew there was something lurking in these woods, if he heard the stories of my people, he knew that I was wicked and that the damned followed me. Stalked me. Almost as much and as well as Banu. He had been on high alert since I had taken his hand that sunny afternoon and run off with him. Pleased and even thrilled that I had taken the first step to be with him—for only two days, anyway—and yet he was also cautious and wary of the dangers it meant when I was with him. If something were after me, he wanted to be the one to protect me. Better for me to have the hunting knife so he could be the one to capture and kill the spirit that was after me.

It wouldn't work. That is not how you kill a spirit. Everyone knew that smoke and fire warded off the spirits. But Banu wouldn't listen. He believed he could protect me. I didn't argue with him, let him be foolish to think those things. It would not harm him, after all. The evil spirit was after me.

As a child, we roamed the open forest together, sleeping in a new spot almost every night. He would tell me that it was not safe to always sleep in the same spot night upon night. That gave predators a good idea of where we would be, the information gave them the knowledge to stalk and ambush us. I do not remember all the little nooks and crannies we had hidden in.

These last two nights we have slept in a cave.

Through the cave opening, I could see SunFather's light bright and strong, lighting the foliage. Bright green leaves hung down over the opening of the cave. The dank odor of the cave blends with the cologne and musk of Banu's scent and my own.

Inside the cave I wait. Banu had left earlier and had told me to stay. He had heard something in the distance and said he senses something different on the wind. A new taste to the leaves and the sweet aroma of the jungle. I could not taste that or sense it, but in the past he had always been right about these things.

There is a rustle outside, a stirring. Then a flock of screaming birds in the distance. I strain to hear. Silence, deep and total. It is unnatural.

Where is Banu?

I am not one to hide. I do not fear the forest or the animals that lurk in it. I do not even fear the stalking spirit. Fresh birdflesh dance across my skin. Shivering, I rub at my arms and wait. And wait. Noises sounds outside. Snapping of dried twigs.

"Banu?" I ask. It must be him.

Tentatively, I step outside, shielding my eyes from the bright glare of the sun when a red and angry jaguar springs; but the ledge it is come from must have eroded with time and mud for it breaks under the cat's weight and its leap falls short. I scream and draw out the hunting knife. It backs away, sensing danger coming from me when it turns to attack with lightning speed.

In its yellow eyes I feel the power of the animal. Majestic and far stronger than an ordinary animal. I sense its power.

It is a spirit animal!

And with that awareness I sense my father's thoughts. That momentary connection stops me for the briefest of seconds.

A fierce pain stabs my chest as its claws pierce my skin.

Oh no! I will die from these wounds.

I try to slash with the hunting knife into the jaguar's flank, but the knife slips and only grazes its side.

It screams in pain, a fierce roar, an angry sound and then bites into my shoulder. I see the bite coming, the glistening yellow stained teeth and I feel that it will go for my throat. I quickly twist, a turning of the body, my shoulder catches the animal on its maw.

Agony floods me. I scream out in pain, echoing the cry of the cat.

My bruises from three days ago were just beginning to heal. Tears fell from my eyes and my fingers scratch at the ground for the hunting knife.

Where is it?

Shadow descends from the sky as a dark swirling mass flew

from the jungle, knocking the jaguar off of me. Its teeth wrenches from my skin as it flies backwards. I lay on my side as I see it land and it immediately jumps up to attack the intruder. A black panther stands over me, teeth bare, its hackles raise on it back. It is so close to me that I could see every strand of its sleek black fur. I can smell its musk. Its tail twitches violently.

I spot the knife. *It's just a few feet away!*

I crawl towards the knife I have dropped when the jaguar bit me again. Its teeth barcly make contact and I realize that it's just a grab as the jaguar attempts to steal me away. I feel its body fling backwards as the panther claims me for his own.

With my good arm I reach out, my fingers prodding at the weapon. A fight in strews behind me. Both animals roaring and screaming in anger. Both wanting me. My shoulder seems to not want to function as my fingers on my left-hand ball into a fist—I think my shoulder is broken, and I shove off the ground with my knees and promptly fall face first into the ground.

Screams erupt behind me as the animals fight for their prize. Blood splatters onto my skin but I do not flinch away from the gore.

The knife.

I must get to the knife!

It is my only hope.

I moan out as my shoulder pains me—I can barely move. Only my knees keep me crawling forward. "Oh Banu! Where are you?"

I see the black cat turn and stare at me, probably confused or wondering why the easy meal has suddenly started making noises again.

"I am not a meal for either one of you!" I shout into the dirt.

The red jaguar with its large mouth jumps for the black's throat. Like a shadow billowing through the fog, the panther jumps to the side and then springs off the ground with its powerful hind legs and goes for the red.

Both spirit animals fight like nothing I had ever witnessed before.

Never in my life have I faced so much danger as I have right now. To be so vulnerable. My father has my bow and arrows and my very own hunting knife. My fingers finally clutch around the hunting knife that was Banu's. If I will die, it would be on my feet with a little something from my friend.

I will face this assault like all the ones I have faced before!

As the shadow cat chases the jaguar from its meal, I make a choice. I rose to my feet and lurched after the panther. The shadow cat stops at the end of the clearing and roars at the retreating jaguar. I can see the jaguar staring at me, filled with hate and loathing and something else, a jealous gleam in its eyes that I do not understand. As the panther roars, I imagine myself hearing its thoughts, "Do not ever come back! This is my place! She is mine!"

His? That is silly. It only wants me for his own to eat me. To be food for its empty belly.

Why do I argue with myself over the word, "mine"? Of course, the panther believes I am his. He has fought off an angry giant jaguar and now I am his dinner. Yes, of course, I am his.

But not if I can help it!

My feet pummel into him. He crouches, ears lay back onto his head as he turns and stares at me with green eyed horror. My knife rises into the air—and the shadow cat leaps forward and runs away—just as my knife plunges into the earth where his heart would have been. I fall forward. Tears flood down my face as my shoulder screams out in pain and something else… a feeling in my heart feels torn.

Weeping. Always weeping. What is wrong with me lately?

A gush flows between my legs and I simultaneously feel the onsets of cramps in my lower back.

That is when I started my moon flowering…

Why does moon flowering always come at the least expected time?

13

"Why do these things happen to you?" Banu asks. He arrives shortly after I have chased away the black panther. He looks confused and even a little hurt when he sees me. His eyes fall to his knife in my hands; I have not released the weapon since I was able to grasp it in my palm. Then he saw my shoulder and immediately helps tend to it.

I should not be surprised when he kisses my wounds gently before touching it with his fingers.

He is strange—almost as strange as me.

His hands are always so warm, and I knew that he could be gentle at times—the riverbank showed that to me—but now it felt like claws touching my skin.

"Owwww!" I groan at him. "Can't you be a little more gentle than that? I am hurt."

"I'm sorry. I am being as gentle as I can. We will need to clean this thoroughly. A jaguar's bite is not clean. And I see you have puncture wounds on your belly. I need to see those too."

"I hurt all over. Like being thrashed by my father all over again."

"I don't understand why the jaguar came for you. Did you leave the cave?"

"Of course, I did. I thought it was you out there. I heard something—thought it was you—called your name and heard more noises."

"I told you to stay inside. It was not safe."

"How was I supposed know that? You just ran off, said you sensed something wrong."

"I did. Look at you. You could have been killed. You really are forming a habit to be saved."

"Just to remind you, you did not save me this time." I hold out my finger, pointing as I spoke. "I scared off that panther. It was me. It ran off because of me." I am proud of the steel of my backbone, to face the very thing that had been stalking me all this time. Again, my heart gave a lurch as though something is wrong with that thinking.

Banu looks taken aback or mildly uncomfortable. "Yes, I suppose you are right."

"How is it you lived in the woods for so very long and have never had an issue with the jaguars and caiman?"

He shrugs, still looking uncomfortable. "You are not always around, Ara Macao. These scars on my body were not founded by me playing around. You are lucky you were not there to see those fights occur." He does not need to point at his arms, chest and shoulders. It was true, he was covered in small nicks and that have healed into fine scars.

"Banu," I begin. "What was it that you sensed? Was it the jaguar? Normally you have been good about danger and where it comes from. How were you so far off this time?" Asking makes me feel discomfort, like as if I do not trust Banu's judgement. It is not my meaning to come across as if I distrust his discernment.

He looks uncomfortable. Still. As if he is having trouble with his own thoughts. Usually he always makes me feel anxious but now I see that I am rubbing off on him. "There was something else I sensed. It turned out to be nothing. For now, anyway."

I cock my head and looked at him curiously. "What do you mean there was something else? And what do you mean it was nothing, for now? Is there something we need to be worried about in the future?"

"Everything?" A smile tugs at the corner of his mouth.

"Ah," I say nodding at him. "Such wise words from Banu, boy of the forest and tender to grave wounds."

He chuckles and motions for me to follow him back into his little cave.

"Why are we going in there? I thought you wanted these wounds to be cleaned?"

"I do," he says tersely.

"And inside this cave you have a great well of healing water?"

"I might," he says.

I squint my eyes at him but continue to follow him. I trust Banu. Even if this turns out to be some rues or a prank, I would continue to put my faith into my childhood friend.

The darkness of the cave seems absolute as my eyes adjusts to the dim lighting. I stand near the entrance as Banu moves towards the back of the cave. I see that he is searching for something, but I do not know what. Not long, he comes forward with something small in his hands.

"Come, let's go into the light where I can see you better. You smell of blood, too much for my nose to understand."

"I will need to clean myself," I say. There is blood, more than just bites and the claws had made. Warm liquid trails down my leg. I will need to clean myself and see to my moon flow. "Banu, where do you take me?"

"You smell," he says to me, with a wry smile. "I think you are a mess. I think it is time to clean you up. I'm taking you to a place to get you smelling just a little better. If only just a little better."

I chuckle. "Seriously, Banu, I need to clean myself. I think I can go to the river and wash off."

"The river is not safe. You smell like blood and you will become a target for other predators. There is only so much I can do to keep you safe, why would you want to tempt animals to hunt you?"

I had not thought of that. I am wounded. I hurt all over.

These wounds, though they hurt me, I can see that they will attract those things that might want to eat me. Especially the small pesky ones such as flies. Banu is right. I don't think the river is a good idea. Not only will it might attract more jaguars, but I may attract the notice of my people. It is kind of strange, actually. I have not seen anybody in these woods while I have been with Banu. My mind begins to wonder, where did all the people go? And, what did Banu sense earlier? I will find my answers soon enough, though I have a feeling that I will not like what I find.

"It is just over here," Banu says. "It is well away from everything that may try to kill you."

"Are you going to tell me what it is that you carry?" I have tried to think what is in his hands. It looks like a coconut shell that has been cracked open, split in half. What would he need with the coconut? How will that help my body heal and clean the wounds from my flesh before the mean spirits enters my body and makes me sick? Or predators became attracted to all the blood pooling down my legs? So many questions pops into my head. I feel that it is a safety mechanism, so I do not think about all the blood and my light-headedness I am feeling. Or the stiff shoulder I refuse to move less I fall into darkness of agony with any movement.

I cradle my arm, so it does not swing, careful not to touch the punctures marks to my belly. I see red. Lots of red. The blood was not only just from the moon flowering, the wounds from my chest and stomach bled gently. And they are beginning to throb with pain.

"You will find what is in my hands soon enough," he says, without looking at me. Well that is good to know. Banu sometimes aligned the mysteries of the sky to keep his secrets from me. He is, after all, a forest boy. He has his own powers that not even I could fathom. I wonder why he would keep something from me right now. I am hurt, the least he can do is ease my mind.

"Well thanks a lot," I say to him. "You sure know how to put my mind at ease."

"I try my best with you. Though, I think you like to test it."

"What can I say? You did say you were going to protect me."

He seems to bristle at my words. His jaw muscle tenses, and

I could see that my words have stung him. He has given me his word that he will be there to protect me. To make sure that no harm comes to me. After all, he did invite me into the woods with him for two days. To keep me from other men so they do not claim my body, claim my soul for the taking.

My cheek flare with heat with the implications of his intentions.

He wants me for himself.

He wanted to protect me from others. Yet I have been injured by a spirit jaguar while he was out trying to find the danger that he sensed. I could not help but wonder, if perhaps the danger he has sensed had been the jaguar all along. *Maybe that is why he is so upset right now?*

He had thought the danger had been far away and yet the danger had only been a few feet from where we had slept. Maybe he was seeing the error of his ways, maybe he knew that he could not protect me.

I do not need his protection, anyway.

I have not needed anybody since I was a little child. Though I take comfort in knowing that I have a friend, at least one friend in this world and I am glad it is him. But I do not expect him to protect me all the time just because he is my friend. Maybe, one day I could try to protect him. You know, even the score a little bit in my favor.

"It is over here," he says to me. "Please sit by the spring and let me see to your injuries."

"You want me to sit right here by the water?" We have entered into a gentle clearing with a small pool of clear beautiful water. I have not been here before. Though I admit, I have not been all over the forest, I have only been where Banu has taken me, taking his word for what is safe and off limits.

He told me that I should not wander randomly all over the forest. Those were good words to go by. Animals and not just the dangerous animals were these wood. But the people too, claim the forest as their home so it is only right to take care where you put your feet. Not only did my village live here but other peoples as well.

"Yes, it's right there, by the water," he says. "And let me take a look at you."

"I stopped by the water, careful not to stick my body into it." It is bad luck to be by water while injured, as it tempts water spirits to come out of the water to claim your body as their own. Everyone knew this, but Banu, clueless as ever, ignored what everyone should know by being… well… Banu.

I hurt and am covered in blood, not just blood from the injuries but the blood that was corrupted. Sinful blood. A woman's blood. Blood pouring during the purification process a woman's body did so to purge herself of evil. Men did not need this as they hunted and would bond spirit animals with their trials. Women bled their sins.

And I was experiencing my moon flowering. Blood, I had not seen in a long time since my first bleeding when I became a woman.

The moon flowering.

Ordinarily, most girls start their moon flower when they became a woman at the round twelve years old to fifteen years old. I had my first flowering when I was eleven. And I have not seen my flowering since. Occasionally when the other girls would get their flowering, I would also get the symptoms of pain and discomfort that they felt. Yet, no blood drizzled down my body. It is one of the reasons why some men thought me unwholesome to have as a woman as a pair bonded mate, for fear that I could not become with child. And the shaman thought I had evil accumulating in my body.

Many believe that is why I am so wicked.

However, it runs in my family to not flower as often as other women. Before my mother had children, she only got her flowering once or twice a year. This goes for my grandmama as well. And for many years my mother has not had a flowering. She believes her baby days are over even though she is only turning thirty soon. A young age to stop moon flowering.

I watch Banu come around to my side and his hands brushes my shoulder, not my injured one but my whole shoulder. His rough, warm hands caresses my skin. It is not a sign of passion like my mind would have thought days before. It was a sign of comfort of a healer about to tend to the wounds of the one that are injured. I took comfort in his touch as I always did. I relish his fingers, his arms and body, his face. And I think deep down he knew this.

He comes around to my injured arm and he kneels down low to take a closer look at what the jaguar has done to me during our brief skirmish.

"This is where the Jaguar bit you," he says, as his fingers gently touched me. "I can see where his lower jaw grazes your underarm and snagged you on top of your arm near your elbow. You are lucky that you did not lose this arm. But, it is still a possibility. A jaguar bite is never a clean one. Filthy beasts." Though I saw that he says this last bit with a twinkle in his eye that I did not understand.

It is not funny to me.

I might lose my arm!

"Now this, your chest has claw marks. His claws are not a grievance, after all. Though they have bled, I can see that they have not punctured into your abdominal wall. If that had happened, I might lose you. But it is no matter, it is not something to worry about. It is just superficial. Like being scratched by a branch or tripping on the rock. They need to be cleaned or they will get infected, but this salve can do the trick for that."

Like a branch? Or being tripped? "So, you are saying it's like falling into the water?"

"No, it is not like falling into the water. Water can mean death by drowning by predators. This is like getting a scratch. You are lucky the claws did not pierce you as badly as they could have. Jaguars are Panthers number one rivals in the forest. They hunt the crocodile and the alligators. They fear little. They think they are so much better than the panther."

I look up at him and see that his face is scrunching up into a curious look. How could he care so much about Panthers and Jaguars? Then I think, why should he not? He is after all a forest boy and he lives with these creatures.

"You didn't think I was that hurt, did you?"

"No," he said, after a moment. "You were able to walk."

His eyes squint down at my legs and he knelt beside me. "What is the wound to all this blood?" he asks me. "I do not see where you are cut."

I cannot help but have a smile that breaks across my

face. "Maybe, you need your face a little closer, so you can see it a little better."

He frowns and begins to lean in, then catches my eyes, stopping himself short.

Pity. I was hoping he would take the bait.

A wicked grin plays across his face. Then he sits up and stares me in the eyes. "I see," he says. "That is why there is so much blood. You have gone into heat?"

Heat floods my face, and I stare at him dumbfounded. "It is not called heat, you idiot. It is my moon flowering."

"I did not think you got those. Is this your first one?"

"No, it is not my first one," I say heatedly, remembering the looks of damnation I receive from my people back at the village. "I just do not get them very often."

"Is that not strange for a woman? I was certain that women tend to get them every new moon. I always thought you did not get them."

I glare at him. At his words of insensitivity. He can be such a stupid boy at times. Saying the wrong things at the wrong times. Yes it is strange that I have not gotten more flowers. But I am a strange girl.

"I do not know how to help you in this," he says to me. A puzzled frown is on his face. He is truly assessing this situation and having trouble coming to understand that this is something he could not help me with.

I chuckle. "It is not something I need help in. But, if you would like to help my shoulder and the rest of my body, I would be grateful. I need these cleaned. And whatever vile thing you plan on putting on me from your coconut shells, that would be fine too."

"Then I am grateful that I can be of service to you." He split apart the coconut shell, and I can see that it was split equally in half. He pulled them apart, and I saw that one side was empty while the other side was filled with a green thick paste.

"What is that?" I sniff the air and smell something pungent; bitter tree sap or crocodile vomit. No, that was not right. I do not believe crocodiles can spit up. But it was something else that I imagine would have a very vile smell, and probably equally distasteful to put in one's mouth.

"This," he says giving me a look, "is medicine."

"Medicine?" I ask him. "How did you get medicine? When have you become a shaman?"

"Shaman are all fake and full of platitudes. They use things that are natural and treat the natural like the supernatural. This here is just a bunch of mulched up herbs and saps that are known to help treat wounds."

"I have never heard of such a thing. I think such things are forbidden in the village. Except, when the shaman makes it."

"See what I mean? You are all under the influence of a man who collects much power."

"What do you mean? I have never heard of you speak about the shaman before. Here, I thought you just disliked my father."

"I loathe your father. I equally detest people of false spirituality." With the coconut shell that did not harbor the green bitter smelling paste, he fills it with water from the spring and begins to trickle it over my wounds. Dried blood softens and sloughs away. The waters splash down my cuts and scrapes, stinging initially as it touched my pained skin. As the orange color of newly wet blood begins to trail down my body, the water begins to fee refreshing, too. I long to go swimming in that water with my friend. And briefly, I wonder if this was the spring he had wanted to bring me many days ago.

"Careful not to get my blood in the water," I say to him.

"It will go downhill, do not worry," he says to me. Then he paused and stared at me bemused.

"What?"

"Another one of your people's superstitions? Fearing blood in water?"

"I do not want to poison this water and kill all the fish."

He chuckles. "There are no fish in this water. It is a spring from the mountains. That is why it is so cold."

"Maybe someone had already poisoned the water with blood," I suggest.

He shakes his head in disbelief. "No, that is false. It is this evil spirituality that makes man not rise up to his full potential. So much false spirituality to control people's minds."

False spirituality? Control? I did not understand these sudden things he was saying to me. From the look in his eyes, I could see that he believes what he says.

That is the scary part. He believes in his own lies. How can anyone defy the spirits and the ancestors and what they teach?

Deftly with his two fingers he applies paste to his hand and then gently applies the thick green stuff to my skin. It is cool as it touches my skin and give a pleasurable tingling sensation as it sits. I would have thought that such a disgusting smelling concoction would burn when applied.

"Yes, it is cool," I say, in comment to the spring being so cold. "I thought the paste would burn when being smear onto my skin, but it does not. The wounds are not experiencing the fire I thought would happen. Maybe the wounds are not infected after all."

"If they were, you would not like the sensation as the medicine suck out all the poisons that might've been entered into your body."

"This medicine can do that?"

"It can. You probably do not remember, but long ago when you live with me for one whole month. I used this on your knee."

"Oh, that was what was used on my leg? I had nearly forgotten." A long time ago when I was almost 6 years old I lived with Banu in the forest for the entire moon. A period of a month. I have been shunned and banished from my village because they thought I had lied about the forest dweller. That I was playing tricks on the people. Using their good will to my evil ways. The shunning and then banishment were supposed to kill me. If they did not—and they hadn't—they were seen as a fitting punishment.

Not many people have been banished. Never a child. And I survived.

"What do you use for the moon flowering blood?" he bursts out. It was not a subject that men liked to speak about. The color red was seen as a life giver whereas the color white was death. Men killed and drained the blood of their prey—our meat—and returned with a pale carcass. When live animals were brought to the village, men would do the killing blow, but it was the women who cleans up the blood. For they gave life. Red the color of life.

The same for dead animals. A woman could not handle the dead. A male relative or villager, had to carry the corpse of a loved one to the pyre before it was lit. For the color white is death and a woman's body is that of life. To mix the two brought evil into the world.

It was one of the rumored my mother had touched her dead sister when she was pregnant—though it could not be proven—thus I was born as I was. Wicked.

"Usually," I say to him, stiffly, with an edge to my voice. "We sacrifice one of the young unpaired and drink the milk from their bones. Then we use their bones to craft our tools."

His mouth fell open. Complete slack jawed. He had not been expecting that answer.

It was my turn to smile at him. I feel like I am evening the score between us. After years of him getting the better of me, am I finally racing to the top?

"We don't wear anything, usually. But I have seen women use grasses if they are going to be walking about. But usually women all go into the wigwam. it is a time of spiritual and bodily cleansing. There were times almost every single woman was in there, letting their blood pool on stones. Stones later used to catch river fish."

"I thought the blood would kill fish," he says, pointedly.

My mouth must have thinned to a line as I glare at him. He really can be obtuse! "We let the blood dry first. It is fine then. It is no longer fresh!"

"What about the crafting? Cooking? The children? Who takes care of all of these things when the women are experiencing their moon flowering?"

Sometimes, I forget that Banu has never lived with people before. He does not know the ways of the people. "Very young children would be with their mothers. The other older children are watched by women whose moon flow has not come. Or they are watched by the elderly women. It is why women past flowering are favored amongst the women of the village."

Banu sighs. "That all makes sense. So, you have several shabonos for every family? Is there only one wigwam?"

I breathe out patiently. He doesn't know. How could he know? "We have four main shabonos at the center of the village. They are the original families that started the village. Then there are the eight shabonos surrounding those. Another five to six families per shabono."

"That is a lot of people."

"You've seen our village. It is the pride of these mountains and the people of these forests. With more people arriving to our village every day, there will be another eight shabonos erected to house the newcomers."

His face scrunched up. "Those are the women and children that have been arriving to the villages?"

"Yes," I tell him. His face darkens, and he looks… guilty?

"What's wrong?"

He swallowed, looking at his hands. Hold the two shells, one in each. Then he brought them together, closing the halves to become whole once more.

"Your village will have a lot more mouths to feed. There are so many more women and children now. Not enough hunters to feed everyone."

"We will manage. We always do."

Quietly, he says to me, "We cannot have you walking the forest with blood falling freely, it will attract predators."

"I know." I sigh. "It is time for me to return to the village. Maybe with my moon flow, my people will see me as a woman of power and honor. My body is purifying itself of toxins and evil."

"The lack of your moon flowering causes the distrust?"

I nod. "Some of it. While the women bonded together every month, I got to run free. And I refused to do their chores. They never helped me with mine, anyway."

He chuckles. It was dry and did not hold humor. "Not much of a team player, are you?"

"Can you blame me?"

"No. I don't. In fact, I would have done the same if I were in your feet. They had no right to treat you so poorly. Well then, that's the last of the ointment. I'll need to gather more herbs and mulch them. Your wounds should heal fine."

My skin looked to be covered in green smears. People would see the wounds and wonder how I survived an attack against a jaguar. They would see the wounds and see the green and remark on it. Only the shaman could create healing medicines.

"Thank you Banu for tending to my wounds. I do not know where I would be without you in my life."

"In a village, surrounded by people you hate. Or drowned in a river, ignored by the people who hate you. Or," he says, grimly, "you would have died ten years ago in the forest, all alone."

I nod sagely. He is right after all.

"Let's get you back to your village. I would not want a hunter to be attracted to you by the scent of your moon flowering."

We rise to our feet—Banu standing first and then helping me to mine. Blue light catches my eye as SunFather's light reflects off the water. The water looks so clean, so refreshing. I would have loved to have taken a dip in that water, but I did not want to pull a strand from my head and tie it to a branch nearby. I will be losing hair after I return, and my father saw to me. And—I admitted; I do not want to wash away all of Banu's hard efforts at applying the healing salve to my winds.

We turn and leave the peaceful pool of bright waters, heading back to my village.

14

Following the game trail that circles down the cliff, we headed back towards the village. The shaman said that the water traders will come soon.

Today will be the day that they arrive.

For the past two days I have enjoyed my time with Banu, and sadly it is coming to an end. But, it did not mean that I will be finding a mate. It has been two days already. And my people would think I am dead.

Oh, my poor grandmama.

She had seen me fall into the river because I tried to go after the fish that had caught her foot, she did not see my forest friend coming to save me. She had run off to the village to try to find help. I hope she has not suffered too greatly during my days away.

The people think me dead and my body feels like it. My shoulder throbs with each step, but as we draw nearer the village, the fire in it begins to lessen.

I can face them. I would face them and what would come.

They thought me dead and now I come back; they will think me a spirit. With my friend at my side, I will do this. I will face the wrath of my father because he will want to prove that his spirit and his spirit animal is stronger than my own. That he can keep a wicked child like me from rising up. No, not a wicked child… But a wicked woman.

What would the people think with my friend at my side? Banu. I cannot believe he was actually going to come with me to the village. When I had asked him how far he would walk me to the village, he had told me that he will take me all the way. He wants to make sure that I will be all right when returning.

"Banu you do not have the come with me. I know you dislike being surrounded by so many people."

"I know," he says. "But it is as I had said to you, I will take you to your village and there I will make sure that they do not harm you. You have your moon flowering; I want to make sure that you will be all right."

"You will let the people see you?"

He shrugs and I can see that he doesn't look very uncomfortable like I thought he would be at the prospect of being surrounded by so many. He has lived in the forest for so many years since he was a child, since I was a child. Could he handle being around so many people? How will the introductions go? I feared that he would become anxious. I know I do when around so many. And with his dark skinned and my dark skin… We may appear as spirits walking forth from the forest and the people would not be pleased. These thoughts worried me.

"I can also hide from them, if I choose to. I can hide in your village as you return, and they will not see me. Would you prefer that?"

I am dubious that he could pull that off successfully. They were many—and my village had a few dozen men that were aged hunters. They would spot him if he tried to hide. "Only if you want to. These are my people. I know they do not treat me well and seeing you at my side, I just worry that they may think us to be spirits."

"Your people are filled with superstitions. I hope that one day they will see you for who you are. For who I see you to be."

"And how do you see me?"

"I see you as a beautiful woman, strong and resilient. One who has faced troubles all of her life, unjustifiable troubles."

"We cannot change people's minds, Banu. We have to show them that we are who we say we are. Who we would like them to see us as?"

"And I hope they will see you not as a demon coming in disguise."

"That is very nice of you, but I wonder, what would they think of you when they see you?" It was supposed to be a jab. A joke between us but by the frown on his face I could see that he also wondered that too.

"Come on, let's go, we are almost there," he says to me. With him at my side, my feet no longer hear, the pain in my shoulder and the rest of my body seemed to lessen. With the sun on our skin, we headed towards the hillside of the village.

THE VILLAGE WAS JUST UP AHEAD. I AM ALWAYS SURPRISED AT THE strength and fortitude of my people. When something happens, we rise up. When too many guests come we over prepare meals. When a woman gives birth at the same time as another, we are ready for it.

My eyes set upon the village.

I can see several new family homes have been constructed in my absence. Working together men and women both from my village and women who had come searching for new homes when their villages had been faced with demons; constructing new homes for the families.

I do not understand what happened to these people. The shaman has said that we would be expecting new arrivals from people's outside of our village, other villages of the forest. It is a little scary to think about it, outsiders. But they are of the people. They are my people's. We welcome them with open arms, our generosity is felt in my heart, felt throughout everyone's hearts.

I can smell fire, and meat roasting on the spit. Fresh melons and mangoes that have been cut up recently wafted with the aroma of cooking meats. Cut grass and wood mingle in my senses. And most of all the smell of my people.

This is my village. The village on the hills, surrounded by forest and to one side the cliffs, the other side the ocean. It is growing. With over sixty families with several children of their own and all the outsiders that were to come, our village was growing. It has grown so much over the last fifteen years of my life.

And look at all the children!

I can see children playing. Dozens of them. Boys and little

girls, mostly naked, running around with sticks dragging on the ground or chasing each other. Probably playing at hunting and gathering. They are old women nearby watching these children play, their gnarly fingers weaving a basket or other crafting materials together made of thatch and dried grass, woven with soft fibers. I do not recognize some women, for they must be new to our village. They had the looks of the traveling of great distance. Bags beneath their eyes, those red eyes.

They are grieving.

I wonder what has happened to these people. A demon in the woods? The same one that had stalked me, the same that I had chased away. Or was it something else, something truly evil? What were they running from or what was chasing them?

And most of all… Where were the men? The husband's, the father's, the brothers.

All I could see was women and young children. Where were all their men? Not even grandfathers were present.

"I think," Banu says at my side, "that maybe we should not be seen right now." He looks unusually pale as he witnesses the grief of these strange women.

"Why do you say that?"

"I think there is something that you should see."

I squint my eyes at him, not understanding. "Okay. Fine. But I cannot be made to linger. I have to let them know that I am still alive. If they see me lurking in the shadows before I return, it will not be good for neither one of us."

He grunts in reply and says no more. Hunching over ourselves we make our way, behind the family homes. Voices could be heard coming from the center of my village. That was not unusual whenever gatherings were held it always happens at the center of the village.

But… I cannot help but wonder, *why are they gathered?*

As we edge our way closer, I can see many bodies standing together talking amongst themselves. Women sitting together, something had caught their attention. But who? Or what?

"I think we should go no farther," Banu says.

"What do you think is up ahead?"

"I don't know," he says to me. "Something smells strange. It is a smell I smelled her earlier."

My eyes widened at him. His sense of smell was always extraordinary to me. I have always wondered if he has a spirit animal that he did not tell me about enhancing his human senses. "Something you smell. That is why you ran off earlier?" I have an uneasy feeling forming in my gut.

Through the dried grasses and sticks sitting in a pile, towards the bodies of the people, I could see cooked meat on a spit at the fire. Not just meat from a bore but spits of small morsels; bird perhaps roasting. And something larger. Very large. Caiman. We normally do not have caiman. They are very dangerous to hunt and to kill.

When near the river, if you saw one in the water you can be sure that there were dozens others beneath the surface stalking you, waiting for the unwary to step a foot onto the murky river bottom so powerful jaws could snatch and pull the unwary beneath the water. In the two days since I have been gone, a lot seems to have happened.

And then I saw them.

New arrivals.

People not from the forest. The traders from the water. They were few, as my people outnumber them. They were far taller than the tallest man in the village. I was amongst the tallest in the village nearly looking into my father's eyes and he was very tall. And yet, these people, these traders from the water, were so much taller than even him. I glance back at Banu and looked back the strangers from the waters and believe that only my friends would be as tall as these foreigners. And the shaman who was unnaturally tall.

The traders tower over my people like trees over the growing shoots. Fair of skin, and in my case much fairer than mine, with hair of a variety of colors. I have never seen hair those colors before. The Reds the color of the flying birds. Browns like a variety of tree bark growing in the woods never one color or shade. And yellows, varying from dark yellow of the crocodile's belly to the dry pale color of cut grass. Most people in my village have dark brown hair the color of river mud. Some have glossy black hair, the color of wet river rock.

Then there is me. I have black hair like a panther. Thick and wild.

Even from this distance, as I see them towering above my father and other warriors of the village, I can see that they are covered in thick beards in the shades of the hair colors on their heads. Their eyes are not brown or black like my people's, theirs shades of green like my own.

At the center, between all the tall men, is one man who must have been in charge. The leader amongst the traders from the waters. He has on a weird looking thing on his head. They are all strange to look upon.

My people see these people as divined traders from the waters, but I only saw them as strange. I do not trust them. They are too different. The way they looked at each other with the same amount of distrust that they looked at us. Something in their stance. The way they behaved.

How can no one see this but me? I must be losing my mind. As I stand here watching them, I see large boxes, crates sitting alongside the shabonos. Those must be the things the traders have brought from the water. I look around and for the first time, I notice some of my people were adorned in white silky shirts that looked strange on their tanned skins. There were blankets and other items that I could see from those opened trunks. I narrow my eyes at the gaudy possessions that they had to trade.

But how can we afford the trade when we have no hunted for the white or gold stones that these people seemed to like?

Banu tenses at my side, sensing my suspicions.

"Lots of dead bodies heading up this way." The man in the red and black breeches says. He was the one with the weird thing on his head with a feather sticking out. The leader.

He speaks our language fluently with very little accent. Banu frowns, probably thinking the same thing.

"Dead bodies?" My father asks. He is bare chested, and his skin was lean with muscles that could only be required as a man who hunted regularly. I saw a few nicks and cuts on his chest… those were new.

"The women and children who have come from distant villages," the shaman spoke up from my father's side, "have told us of how their men died while on their travels to our village. It is a horrible thing. A travesty."

The leader of the strangers eyed the shaman and my father skeptically. Oh, how he was suspicious of us. "These bodies looked like they were attacked by a monster. Do you guys have monsters in these woods?"

"It is unfortunate," the shaman says. "That you have come across these bodies. We will need to find them and send their souls back to our ancestors before it is too late. If it is not already too late."

"I respect that. I have never seen the like before. Where I come from we do not have animals that hunt people."

"Yes, our forests are dangerous," my father says. "But even animals do not kill like this. I'm afraid that it was the works of an untamed beast."

"What do you mean? They're just dead bodies. How do you know what killed them? It look like an animal attack to me. Or the work of savages."

"Animals eat their food," my father says. "And we eat the animals. There is no waste in the forest. It is eaten or be eaten. And what you have told us means there is a demon lurking in our woods. We had hoped it would have been dispelled with… well… no matter."

"I am sorry you have come at the wrong time," the shaman says. "We had a girl die a few days ago. I fear it is her spirit."

The leader frowns and crosses his arms. He had sat down on a trunk when they had begun to talk and is now leaning casually back against the shabono. "That is all right. My men and I are plenty and we are strong. We will be watchful of this demon. You know what it looks like or what she looks like?"

The shaman shakes his head. "If it is the girl, she would not take her bodily form for it was a physical essence. If it is her, she would be in the body of the Black Panther."

"How do you know this?"

"Because the girl was my daughter," my father says gravely. "And she harbors the spirit of a very powerful animal. The black panther."

"I'm sorry for your loss. I too have a son. He is my last child."

"Hopefully your wife can bear you more sons," my father says. My father has never been able to father sons. My mother could only bear females. Daughters. It was the same for my grandmama. It was something many of the women in the village faced. It is why many men in the village would take on more than one woman as a mate. I don't know why my father thought that when he took my mother for mate, that he would make her bear him a boy.

Sometimes, I feel that he resents me. Not for my skin color or my green cat eyes but for not being born a boy. I think he could have overlooked my dark skin and green eyes if I had been a boy. Without a son he cannot pass down his leadership to his next in line. Instead, he has to train Caboko for that role.

"I do not think I will have any more sons. My wife took ill last winter and unfortunately she is no longer amongst the living."

"I am sorry for your mate," my father says. His face looks mournful and regretful. I have never seen my father look sorry before, but I suppose when I am not around he allows himself to show his emotions.

The stranger nodded his thanks. "If we can be of use, my men and I can help track down this monster for you."

"No! It is not safe for you people. You come from the seas

and don't know our ways. You might cause more harm to yourselves and to us by delving in matters you do not understand."

The leader folded his arms across his chest and looked at Zakopelli. "I can understand that. Where we are from, we have laws and rules, too. Not everybody can go do as they see fit even if they wanted to. If there's anything that we can do to help you, please let us know. I mean, we can help point to where these bodies are at so they can be put to rest."

My father nods, he crosses his arms over his thick chest. "I think that would be most kind of you."

That is when one of the tradesmen from the water saw me. With a finger pointing straight at me, he yells something in his own language. Its thickly accented and guttural as if he speaks with water in his mouth or a thick tongue.

"We need to leave," Banu says, and he tugs at my arm, but I pull away from him and stare, transfixed. I see the Shaman staring at me, and it was not he who attracted my attention but the glowing white light emanating from his staff. The spell is over in an instant and I feel lightheaded and dazed.

I blink.

The strangers all turn to face me. Everyone turns to face me. As does my father. There is a collective gasp from all those who are present.

"Spirit Walker!"

"Witch!"

"Black Panther!"

Like a complete idiot, I stand, confused and stare right back at them. I even raise my hand in greeting. That was when a blur zoomed past my face hitting the shabono that I am next to.

When I turned to look, I saw an arrow shaft sticking out from the wall. And my friend is gone. Curiously, I think I see a black blur moving towards the forest.

And that is when my father grabs me by my wounded shoulder and threw me to the ground.

15

A big meaty hand locks onto the wounds on my shoulder, fingers pressing into my skin, as fresh blood pools. I try to retreat but anger and frustration fills me.

For two whole days I have been with my friend, the forest boy and I have nearly forgotten that I would get a thrashing when I returned.

And where have my friend God? Anger boils beneath my skin and my thoughts run wild.

He said he would be there for me, to protect me. What has made him go away? Where has he run off to? He had been right next to me!

He has never been a man to be a coward when I need him the most.

I taste dirt in my mouth as I am thrown to the ground, rolling, I push off my sore side of my body as a foot kicks be in the back. The bruises on my body were beginning to fade, something magical about the forest or being near the forest boy had that impact on me. My father's foot on my skin flare the pain anew.

Bruises that have begun to fade, are in agony. I am in so much pain.

Would I ever be pain-free?

As another foot lands, I scream out in pain and fury. I fervently try to crawl away, back towards the forest, back towards my friend. A pile of twigs and leaves and several branches lay near me and I grab for one. I roll to my back as a shadow looms over me. I hold it defensively in my hands, trying to hold off the attack that I know is coming.

He stares down at me, looking nothing like the papa I have once loved. I groan, clutching at my arm. "Leave me alone, father!"

This is the wrong thing to say to him. If he could have grown more angry than he already is, he would have. His dark eyes are so livid as they stare down into mine. He smirks as he sees me cower at his feet.

"Look me in the eyes, a vile demon," he says.

From where I am at on the ground, I thought I saw something I had never seen before in his eyes. Fright? No, my father had never been so frightened and yet… is he afraid of me? An odd sort of understanding ebbs into my senses as screams and shouts erupt all me.

"Witch!"

"Kill the demon!"

"She will prevent all of us from having babes!"

"Soul catcher!"

These were the voices of the outsiders, of the women who had just arrived. Vile things to say to a woman. If this is what they thought of me... then surely this day is the day I am going to die...

A light shines in my eyes. A light stronger than that of SunFather. A white glow from the black stuff held by Zakopelli. It emanated a soft purple glow.

My father stepped in front of the shaman, shielding me from the light, preventing me from seeing something I should not have seen. I see his fist coming before it strikes me. I groan out in agony as his large fist hits me in the stomach and then strikes me like a serpent as he backhands me across the face. There is blood in my mouth, sweet tang of earthy metals and salt.... Salt from my tears that have fallen from my eyes.

From behind my father, I saw the shaman, Zakopelli. He holds a weird the black staff looking with a holy rock at the end; intertwined with red and blue feathers of our ancestors. It no longer glows but I see his eyes and thought I saw red reflecting from those dark eyes.

A kick to my side has me shut my eyes as a scream bursts from my lungs.

I hear lots of sounds all around me and voices shouting. The familiar and the unfamiliar voices. The traders from the water do not know what is going on. I hear strange noises and I realize that it is coming from the mouths of the strangers.

"Panther!" A guttural voice cries out. More sounds come from these foreigners. They do not understand what is going on or who I am, and the importance of my being here.

Another shadow stands above me.

Oh no...

Not only is my father going to publicly thrash me in front of all of my people, the newcomers and the traders from the water will be aiding in my punishment.

Whimpering, I lower my head in defeat, my long black hair brushes the ground. Dirt touches my lips as I cower before my attackers. Pleadingly, I reach one hand up towards the leathery foot of someone I do not recognize.

They do not pull away. There is not a sound coming from them. Not daring to look up, I reach out my other hand and place it onto his other leg. The materials of his legs, the cloth, is not familiar to me.

I realize it is one of the men from the water.

Pain explodes in my side. I cry out, terrified, and sprawl on the ground willing myself to get up, to move, to face my attackers. Snarling comes from behind me. It is coming from my father. I see him with the sun behind his back, and wetness drips from his fists.

I sigh and lay down on the ground, exhausted, accepting my fate. My father would not stop no matter how much I cry, no matter how much I cry out for help there would be no help to come from my people.

My stare up into the face of the tradesmen. My green eyes stares into his blue. Abruptly, he leans forwards and clutches my father's arm, preventing him from landing another blow to my body. If I could see my father's face I would have been happy. A last and final memory of my father put in his place. I could have died with that.

"Is this your daughter?"

"Daughter no longer," my father says softly. His words rip at my soul. No matter how much he beat me, no matter how much he thrashes me, he will always be my father. But to hear him say those words to an outsider, a stranger not of my people, it shamed me. His words hurt me more than his fists ever could. If he was not my father than my mama was not my mama. What did that make my grandmama? Fresh tears spring into my burning eyes as I catch my father's stare.

His face was blank. Unrecognizable.

"Your daughter is the spirit walker?"

"Yes, this demon is. This is the spirit walker."

"Is she married?" That was a strange word for me as I have never heard it.

"She has not been paired. It has been hard to find someone who is willing to pair with a woman who has works the magic of a demon. She is a wild creature just like the animal that has claimed her."

"An animal has claimed her?"

My father… no… the village leader, for he was no longer my father spoke. "In a sense, yes."

Zakopelli, the shaman came forward. A strange look in his eyes. I have always seen him as a holy man but just then he looked like a man was stumbled across an albino caiman. Everyone knew that animals with white abnormally skin stowed great fortune. To catch one as your spirit animal, you would be lucky for your entire life. And that is how he looked at me just then.

Vaguely, I wonder if he has ever seen Banu, the forest boy?

"She is not pair?" Obviously, the man from the water has never heard of this word before.

"It means she had not had a mate." My father looked at me angrily. Something flashes in his eyes. Hope?

"Why would she not have found a partner?" The man looks

into my eyes, his eyes rove over my skin and I can see that I did not scare him like how I scare my people. This made me uncomfortable. My parents and my ability to keep people away, to keep people from touching me has always been my protection against the world. This man does not look like he cares at all about how I look.

"She is dangerous. Nobody can handle her. She has the black panther's spirit protection. None of our villagers have been able to tame her. The man is judged by his worth of the spirit animal." My father pumps his fist and shakes the blood from his hand. His spirit animal was a jaguar. Equal notch the Black Panther.

"She is very beautiful," the tradesman says with a curiously light in his eyes. "What do I need to trade to have her for my wife?"

I blink in surprise.

"You wish to be her mate?" My father asks.

And I notice that the shaman had stepped up to my father's side. There was a growing hunger in his eyes.

"My wife died last year. Many of my sailors said that I should get a new wife. A younger life. One who would live for many years to come and bear my sons."

The shaman took my father's arm in his own and they share secrets that pass between their eyes. My father is taller than the shaman, for the shaman is old and bent at the spine. In that moment they seem to stand with equal height. The shaman. The village leader.

Something was not right about that. Had the shaman not appeared substantially taller just a short time ago and now he was the same height as my father? A memory tickled in the back of my mind of an image of these two powerful men side by side, and my father had been the taller.

"I think this would be for the best," the shaman says, still looking my father in the eyes. "This tradesman comes from distant waters. Look how tall he is. Look how divine he is. Think not he could take your daughter?"

The tradesman had let's go of my father's arm, he seems to realize that he had been still holding onto it.

My father rubs his chin, a curious light in his eyes. Then he looks at the tradesman, his eyes no longer on me. He stares at the foreigner, assessing the man in front of him. "You wish to have my daughter for mate? As wife?"

"She is very pretty. And I have always liked women of her skin. Her eyes are so green and intense. My last wife was meek. This child before me, would be a challenge to tame. And she has many years to live. She could bear me many children."

My father stands erect, his chest pushed out. "And you know this girl will bear you many children, look between her legs. She has her moon flowering. A good sign that is ripe for babes."

The tradesman grunts. "I can see that." He refrains from looking at my vulnerable state. I can see that everyone in the village and even the foreigners, are watching us. A few people even smile.

"Shaman," the village leader begins. A cruel smile tugging at the corner of his hard mouth. "Did you not say that the first man to enter this village within two days would have my daughter?"

"Yes."

"And has it not been two days."

"Today ends the second day, yes."

"This man before me was the first of his people to step inside the village. Although not of our peoples. He is the first unpaired man to step foot in this village. Is he the one who is in your omen?"

Zakopelli looks thoughtful, as if he had forgotten what he has said. "Yes, I suppose he is the one." He finally said.

"Well then," my father says, with a rare smile broadening his face. "My daughter can be your mate as that is what the ancestors want. For we will see good fortune come of this."

"You do not want to trade? I can bring livestock, animals from our land. I can bring cloths. Foods. Medicines. Anything that you might desire for trade of this woman."

My father shakes his head, only too happy how this is playing out. "No," he says. "The prophecy said the first man to step in this village will claim my daughter for mate. And we would see fortune after a difficult time. It would be wrong to take from you. If you wish to claim my daughter then she is yours to claim!"

I stare up at my father, hating him more than any person I have ever hated in my entire life. If I could move, to get up, to stand up and fight him I would have.

My eyes fall to the pale trader. He is tall and his shadow cast shade over me. I knew that if I deny this man as mate that my father would kill me tonight. There would be no other to stand up against him. Not even my friend, the forest boy could stop the vengeance of my father's wrath at losing the opportunity of pairing off his unfavorable child.

The trader kneels beside me and takes my good arm in his hand and pulls me to a sitting position. And abruptly he leans forward to brush away that hair from my face. It is covered in dirt, as is most of my face. Yet does not seem to care. His blue eyes stare into mine. He grunts his approval and smiles at me.

"My name is Nico Juan Vasquez and you will be my new wife." His eyes fall from my face and slide down my dirty body. This time he allows himself to stare at me. The bulge in his pants surprises me as he stares at me with open hunger. The look frightens me, and I try to pull away from him, but his thick hands are as large as my fathers—if not larger—and he holds me. Traps me in his hands.

Hoots and cat calls erupt from the traders when they realize that their leader was taking a new mate. And that I was his new prize.

A tear slides down my face as hands grab me and pull me to my feet. I knew, by looking at this man that he would take possession of me if he were to have me as mate and that I would never escape him for so long as he lives.

16

S itting in the corner, well away from the others, I listen to their conversations. The walls are dark and made of roughly woven grass fibers. There are slits in the walls to allow natural sunlight and fresh air. This is the Wigwam. The woman's hut. The hut of cleansing. The purification hut. The place where women come the bleed out their sins and evil toxins inside their bodies.

And this was the hut I have been banished to.

I am not alone.

Many of the women sit in conference speaking to one another about the day's events. My sisters were nowhere in sight but their friends and the midwife along with a couple dozen other females from young and old sit in here.

They were my guards. Though they did not know that. Not really, anyway.

These women were having their moon flowering. Same as me. They sit knee to knee in companionship, while I sit in the corner far from them. Far enough away from them where they can keep an eye on me and yet far away enough to not be included in their company.

Tosha, sits next to Okalaki, and they were in deep conversation. I do not know why she is even in here—she was not one of the women who is in her moon flowering. From their furtive gestures with their hands, I knew that someone held a secret. They were all smiles as if someone is pregnant.

Could it be my rival, Tosha? I had not truly meant what I had said a few days ago, that was not right of me. It is not funny to suffer miscarriages or stillbirths. Although I have never had either, I too, have questioned my fertility. And to make another woman question hers, well, that was unkind.

Eyes are on me, causing me to glance away from Okalaki and Tosha to see that Pia and Tuli were looking at me. Maybe, it was because I was looking at their friends.

This was the first time I have ever been included in part of the womanly rituals of life. Monthly moon flowering, the mating rituals, the pairing rituals, and the birthing rituals. All have been excluded from me my entire life. Even when I had started my moon flowering when I was eleven years old only my grandmother and my mama had been happy to sit with me during my first time.

The girls who first receive their moon flowering are carried by the women of the village, into the wigwam where she stays for as many days as needed. Women would sit with her, braid her hair, clean her, make her feel comfortable. The men know when a girl has had her first menses as it is a big deal for a woman. Soon after that the idea of pairing her comes around.

Against my will, here I am. Though at long last I was being

part of something. No one has called me a foul name since entering the wigwam. Women tend to have hot tempers with one another, but it is forbidden in the purification hut. Here we are one. It comes to my surprise that the rule even applied to me.

"Nico," I hear Pia say softly. "That is the man's name."

I hold my arms against my chest. "Yeah, that is the man's name."

"He is strange," Tuli says just as quietly.

Nicolás Vázquez Flores does not seem like a bad man besides my dislike of him. I do not trust him and yet I do not know why that is. He does not see an evil man. In fact, he seems better than most of the men in my village. He had stopped my father from beating me.

He is an unusual person. I like things that are different about people. But I did not want to be with him.

The man is not bad looking for a foreigner, in fact, many the women might even think he is quite charming. Women liked strange and unusual men. It is why when our village traded with others, only the paired were allowed to be around the newcomers unless the person had made known they were mate seeking. Sometimes that happens.

This foreigner, this stranger from the water, is odd looking. He has a strong square jaw and large cheek bones. These traits were desirable to women.

It does not change the fact that I do not want him.

I do not care that I have never had a mate before and that I should be feeling lucky to finally have one. I do not want to make my family and my people happy by pairing myself with a stranger. A person I do not trust.

I knew what they thought. I knew what everyone thought. What they wanted. They do this only for their own satisfaction. To be rid of me at long last. To cast me off and to become some other person's burden.

Sometimes, I do not understand myself and why I had returned to the village. I could have stayed with Banu in the forest... but was this not what I had wanted? I returned to my people. I knew my father would want to beat me. I knew that my people hated me. Yet—why did I return? Something draws me back to the village, back to the desire of wanting to be around people even though I loathe being around people, the crowds and the atmosphere.

I do not want to be anybody's burden. I can care for myself, as I have always done. I constructed my hut, do plenty of foraging for crafting supplies and I hunt all on my own. I have been able to do these things since I was a child. Since my friend... Banu had taken me in for an entire moon cycle. I did not need anybody. In fact, I did not even need my friend Banu.

And he has had left me.

I do not know what has scared him away, but it hurts my heart to know that he was frightened off during my time of need. I need him by my side and without him, I have been relegated as a mate to a stranger.

I should have stayed with him.

He said he would be there for me. To protect me. I have not seen him since he was able to get away. *Maybe he snuck away because he knew the traders would see us... knowing that they would call me a spirit walker and that the village would call me all sorts of vile names?*

I sit alone in this corner where it is dark and unassuming. I listen as the women gossip. Though they do not include me in their conversations, most flat out ignoring me completely, I am able to listen.

"I can't believe it," Tosha says. "I don't think I am ready to have another child. Another pregnancy."

"Just look at those hips, girl, you are ready," Okalaki says at her side. "You have to tell me when you start to get pains or illness as I know the herbs that will aid you. When I am done with my purification process, I will give you these herbs. They will make you stronger. They will make your womb quicken and grow healthy."

"Thank you Okalaki. Caboko has been sending his eagle out to hunt for that rare flower you gave me last time."

"The yellow one?"

"Yes," Tosha says.

"That is very good of him. Smart. Sometimes men lose half of their wits when their woman is with child. Now, be sure not to overdo it with the herbs. And you can take a few other things. Stay away from the river don't lift the waters or anything heavy."

"Thank you, Okalaki, you have always helped me in this. Your herbs are a miracle whereas the shaman just wants to chant with me in a hut full of smoke and ask about butterflies. As If he didn't even know."

"He can be so insensitive," Tuli says. "Your herbs are a life saver."

"It is true," Aba says. "Her herbs are a miracle worker. It is like she is a female shaman."

Abba was a bit of baby boob. She never says the right thing. Unlike me, she can be part of the community, but she never knew what to say. She is the largest woman in the village. She has had many children, two unfortunately have died before their third naming day. Ever since her first child she has always kept on the weight of having babies, never once losing it. Round curves and an impressive bosom. She is quite admiring. I find myself admiring her body, and how she is confident to walk around ready to have another child. She is the mere image of a fertile woman. And her mate took long strides to keep her satisfied. Many women want to be her.

"Aba," Okalaki says, dismissively. "I am not the shaman. You do me an unkindness to compare me to that man."

"Okalaki," Tuli says. "What do you mean by that?"

"Now don't you try to put words in my mouth," Okalaki says with a palm raised. "He is the shaman, not I. I'm just a birthing woman. I know a woman's body. I am not the shaman. The herbs I find are not of men. They are of women. And no shaman can tell me what I can and cannot do with my herbs. Let us see if a man could help a woman give birth. Ha!"

The other women laugh nervously as the fire at the center crackles without mirth.

"I'm sorry Okalaki. I did not mean anything by what I said. I would be very upset if the shaman decided he wanted to birth my babies."

"Men are weak," Zosha says. "They cannot handle blood. Especially not birthing blood. Women are strong. We put up with lots of stretching when pregnant and giving birth."

"Oh, I don't know," Pia whispers, a blush rising to her face. "My man sure likes to stretch me." The women around Pia chuckle and even I smile at that jest.

"Wow look at you Pia. You want to talk more about your man?"

"No," Pia says, hanging her head but I can see a smile on her abashed face.

"I love it when they come back to hunt," Tuli says. "He is always so hard. He comes quickly, but then afterwards… the real fun begins."

More laughter.

Aba makes a weird noise with her mouth as she looks pensive. "You are lucky. My man comes back limp. Like the end of a tapir nose." She holds up her pinky finger and says, "Sometimes this has to be used, too." Then she gives it a wiggle.

Is this what women talk about? I had never been included in part of these female gatherings. I had never heard this kind the conversation before. Ordinarily, women boss each other around. If they have problems with another woman, they make get into a physical fight that barely lasts a minute. Those are rare though they happen. Usually, they argue over who's child is prettiest and whose son is fastest. Whose son will make the greatest hunter. And never did I think I would hear them talk about their men or about sex.

Silence echoes in my ears as I realize their voices caught off. They realize that I have been watching them. I have been taken lax in my thoughts and let my eyes openly stare. I try to look unassuming, innocent but that just makes their eyes furrow.

"All that is right," Tosha says. "Little Ara Macau has never been part of these circles before. She must find the eavesdropping quite entertaining."

"She probably doesn't even know what we are talking about," Zachi says. She is very much like her sister, Zosha.

"Maybe we need to teach her," Abba interjects. "If someone doesn't know something, maybe we need to tell her."

Okalaki rounds on Aba, "We cannot! Her grandmama said it was not time. Only she can sway her mind."

My Grandmama? What did she have to do with this?

"That is a splendid idea," Tosha said and I narrow my eyes at her when I see an evil look in her eyes. "Ara Macao is about to learn a great deal things so that by the time it is tomorrow night, when she and her new mate settle down for the evening, she will be prepared. You will not like it."

"Don't fight him." This came from Abba. She had a wide-eyed look and was nodding seriously. "It will only hurt worse if you fight him."

"Best to lay on your back," Pia says from her knees, arms wrapped around her legs. "Trying not to move your legs or your hips too much as it will pull and tear more."

"Just try to lie still," Abba agrees.

"You have to spread your legs," Tosha says. "And it might help if you kept your mouth shut. It will only keep the men from coming if you talk too much."

"I learned that one the hard way," Aba says. "Except mine just went limp. It was very frustrating for us both."

"Of course, it was. You're such a horn dog," Zachi says.

I stare at them in wide eyed horror. I had seen mating happen in the forest with animals and have overheard mating occur between two paired people and to hear these women talk about this to each other and then to me as if... As if I did not know. I blush.

"If you fight him," Tosha says with a smirk, "he may have to hit you to make your spirit animal submit. Who knows what sort of powers and spirits linger around these strangers?"

Abba bit her lip. "I admit that my man had to make me submit the first time. I was all nervous, and I was laying before him with my legs open and when he came down to me, I got scared and close my thighs. Then I couldn't stop talking."

"You still don't know when to quit," Zachi says, dryly.

"What happened?" Asks Pia.

"He just gave me a slice of dried fruit and then before I knew it he came down at me. It was not fun. Almost wasted a good slice of melon. Sad it was sweet meat, but dried fruit was a pleasantly surprised and reward for that awful task. I did not like it—the sex—the fruit was quite lovely although I had dropped it."

"You are always thinking about food, Abba." Tuli shakes her head. "And sex."

"I think about both equally, I think." Abba agrees.

"As a woman, it is our job to accept the seed of man as that is their job." Zachi says. I blink my eyes at her, she looks and speaks just like Zosha that I can barely tell the two apart sometimes. "It hurts but get over it. It's not the end of the world."

"Well tell us about your experience," Okalaki suggests and as Zachi is about to rebuff her and then she says, "for Ara Macao's benefit. It is her right to know our experiences. She is a woman —look between her legs and see blood. And she will be mated tomorrow. She needs to know." Okalaki then winks at me which catches me off guard.

"My first is a little uncomfortable," Zachi says with a sigh. "I do not think my man knew which one to enter. He used his fingers too much and well—it was fine on my part but every time he wanted to come down it would poke me in the thigh or hip, even the ribs." The women laugh at this, as we as some women not part of the conversation. Zachi takes it in stride. "In the end we did figure it out."

"My man did not know how to take me my first time," says another woman, quietly from the different side of the hut. She had come from a different village, far away. She had a forlorn look mixed with the face of regrets and grief and I knew she was one of the women who had lost her mate. "He made me go on all fours with my backside in the air. He grabbed my hair as he descended. It took a long time for me to take pleasure in that. With our first child my womb quickened very quickly with that method. Try that method if you want a fast quickening."

"I have tried that method," Tosha says quietly.

"Whenever I have been pregnant," Abba says. "My man wants it all the time. He finds it desirable to see me so fertile. Even think sometimes he can do it again to put another one in me while I am pregnant already."

"Men can be odd," Okalaki says. "Very little brains when they have two of them."

"Yeah, my husband was like that too," a woman says.

"Men can be like that sometimes," Okalaki says. "My husband was the same. After my twelve babies, he always believed that he could do it again and again when I was pregnant or immediately after I gave birth. After my first child he would not stop pestering me, so my grandmother and my mother had to sequester me away from him for a while until the birthing blood stopped. As you all may know, it is unsafe to allow men to give you his seed whether you are flowering or having birthing blood. And it might make him sick. We women have birthed lives with ease and know have dealt with the purification process. A man cannot. During our moon flowering, or bodies like go of all the evil inside of us. The same after the childbirth. A child is born beautiful gift from our ancestors. But the blood is corrupted. It is the giver of life. A man cannot handle that. So be careful." Okalaki is like this, always giving helpful advice even when it is not asked for.

They all fell silent with her. I can tell that Okalaki only says these things, not because these women did not know it but because I was there, and she thought me daft and ignorant. She was speaking for me to hear. She may not like me, but she had a duty as a midwife as a birthing woman to convey all that she knew to ensure that the woman was knowledgeable about her body and in the purification process of the moon flowering.

I balled my fist into the ground. The hut was on a hill, the flooring slightly on the incline so that the blood would be carried away from its source, theoretically. The floor was a mixture of coalescing dirt and rocks to provide fresh bedding.

My hands touch the surrounding ground that has not yet been soiled and I realize my fingers were scouring the floor for a perfect color and sized pebble.

Found one!

It rolls between my fingers. Then I pinch it between the nails and skin of my fingers. It was not enough. Deftly, I begin pinching and prodding my skin with the little pebble, jumping between my fingers and diving into my skin in a sort of sweet pain that took my mind off the situation.

Ahh—sweet relief.

I try not to think about just how soiled these rocks might be. In fact, it could be very clean. When a woman is done with her monthly flowering, she will collect the rocks and bring them outside so they can bake in the sun. And then she would go to the river and cleans herself of the dried blood. Since it is dry, it would not harm the fish in the water. And then after she was done with her ablutions, she would collect more rock and stone and bring it back to the village so that another woman would me use the stones. So, in theory these stones could be spotless, or they can be very vile.

I sigh and sit back on my heels feeling the tension in my hips, throbbing pain down into my groin. Occasionally, I feel a little wiggle as blood clots from my flowering removed themselves my body and fall to the ground around my feet. There is no way to be clean. It is an uncomfortable process. When I was eleven years old, my monthly flowering was very… dry. It had not been this wet blood or with clots. It was very dry, and I remember sitting, with my legs spread as I squat down with my mother and my grandmother beside me and no blood dripped onto the rocks at my feet. My mother and grandma joined me for my first flowering, as is allowed for all women's first flowers.

Women could come and go from this hut, bringing food and water for the women having their purification.

The memory from four, nearly five years ago is blurred. Things feel so different now. I am alone and yet I am surrounded by many women in the same process as myself.

I sighed. *I hope my monthly flowering would take another four years to come back.* I do not relish this at all. My muscles in my thighs and lower back are cramped and tradition has it that we should not try to move very much during this time to allow the body to evacuate all the vile that has accumulated. Still, I see women stand and stretch.

Despite being called a witch, a shadow cat, a spirit walker, these women have treated me with respect and indifference. It has the closest I have come to being part of the village… despite the awkwardness of my position I sort of enjoy being around these women. Even Tosha.

Maybe not Tosha…

Vaguely I wondered when the next person would come bearing foods and drink—Tosha had arrived but had not brought anything with her. My mouth felt dry, and the hut feels uncomfortably warm with humidity, heat and smoke from the lit fire in the middle.

As I wait my sentence out until there is no more blood falling from my body, I close my eyes and lean my back against the shack wall. It is warm, and this side faced the afternoon sun. The room smelled of blood and crotch swept. And I had to be in here for as long as blood dripped from down between my legs.

Hours stretched into two days. Women came, and they left. Tosha had left after her conversation with Okalaki and arrive shortly after leaving. She is a silhouette in the doorway until I see her move to me, carrying a small bundle in her hands.

"My mate says these will help your wounds," she says dryly, looking unpleased at delivering her task.

"Your mate? You mean Caboko?"

"Who else do you think? You can be so dumb, Ara Macao. Do you want it or not?"

I hesitate before reaching out and taking the small coconut shell. A memory stirs in me, Banu by the pool of light, tenderly delivering the bitter smelling creams to my skin. A bittersweet memory.

"You look like I just gave you a snake," Tosha says, mouth narrowing to a line. "If you do not want it, then give it back. You need not be ungrateful. My mate went out of his way while collecting me herbs, to make this for you—though I do not see why he would care about you."

"No, no. I want it. Thank you Tosha." As I see Tosha nod and turn away I add, "Well, not you. You didn't go out and get it for me. I will thank Caboko when I am out of here."

Tosha balls her hands into fists but does not look back at me as she marches out of the hut. A chuckle burst out of my mouth until I see the damning eye of Okalaki looking back at me. Guilt floods me, but only just a little.

Many of the women have finished their moon flowerings, with fresh women replace those who have left. Pia, Zachi and Abba along with others were no longer there. A great many women new faces, surrounding themselves with their familiars or stood alone in their purification process, like I do. Not everyone surrounded themselves with people during this intimate time. Some preferred to be alone in a time of reflection, of prayer, meditation.

Of my sister's friends, none were here. My sisters should have had their moon flowering soon. Usually close females all cycled together. Vaguely, I wondered if they even have their moon flowering still. My mama had stopped having her's when she was just a few years older than my sisters. My grandmama also rarely had a moon flowering throughout her life.

Perhaps they are with child. Every woman seemed to get with child. They have mates, after all. And I know that Keira and Kali have tried just as long as Tosha, to become with child, again—their first babies were a few years younger than myself.

Babies. Babies. Babies...

It is what every woman wanted. Why did I not care for having them? I want my freedom, to run where my feet take me, to be in the forest with my friend... I close my eyes and stare up at the tightly woven fibers of the ceiling.

Everyone wants something in life. If they want children, then I hope they get it. I knew that feeling of wanting something and never getting it. I decided that I will think differently—to think differently than the others—if that is what they want, then I wish them all the best. I want my freedom but if they wanted babes, then more power to them. It seems that the women in my village have been cursed, long before I was born, to have very few children, usually more female children than boys.

I just hope that the children look more like me than them when they were born. Then they would understand how I feel. Satisfaction flooded me. Have you babies but let them have what I have so their parents understand how I feel!

No... THAT IS WRONG... I WOULDN'T WANT THAT FOR THEIR babies. Babies are innocent. If only there was a way, I can prove to my people that I am different but no different from they. I think and have wants and have a kind heart too...

How do I go about showing my people that I am not as wicked as they think I am?

I cross my arms feeling miserable. Perhaps, I should stand and walk around for a while, my ankles and knees feel very tight. I have been in this position for many hours since my last stretch and have been enduring this same tedious and rather boring monotone sameness for too long. If there is ever a reason for women to have an emotional outburst, it is justifiable that this is the reason.

I stand and stretch my body, careful not to move too far from my stones. The last two nights of sleeping in here have been uncomfortable. Several times I had woken from my sleep to hear a panther roar in the distance and I hoped Banu is doing all right. Despite my annoyance with his disappearance, I cannot help but feel so utterly alone without him. Abandoned to my fate.

I watch as some women turn over their rocks at their feet like birds fussing over their eggs. That is when I catch the eyes of Okalaki. Again. She seems fixated on me, I decide. I do not want to catch her eyes anymore. Eye contact makes me feel uncomfortable and jittery—I prefer staring at people's noses as it is easier for me. My heart does not jitter as strong when I stare them in the nose. And sometimes, I like to remark on how the nose looks. It makes me feel better with difficult situations.

Okalaki for instance, she is a very strong woman—fit like a man—she can be intimidating when that penetrating look is fixed onto me. When I look at her nose, I feel better. It is square with little wings sticking out the sides. Okay, not precisely like that but those are the things I think about when I stare someone in the face—more precise, when I stare them in the nose. Noses that are pointy, flat, square or maybe large and small. Sometimes I like to look at the nostrils and count the times they move when they brief. You can really tell when someone is getting irritated when the nostrils flare out and the wiggling intensifies. Like right now as I stare at Okalaki's nose, I see it transform into a still moving thing that went from rock to fluid movement like bird wings, flaring with each breath.

As I have said, the hut is very warm as it faces the sun. The smells are strong of old blood and sweat. I sniff and nearly gag. I pull my eyes away from her nose as sense her anger.

Why was she angry?

"Ara Macao," Okalaki begins. I wince at what was to come. A tongue lashing from the birthing woman is never pleasant. The hut grows quiet as they all sense the looming doom. "Why do you hate your sisters?"

The question takes me by surprise. I am not expecting it. In fact, I was expecting anything else but that question.

"I do not hate my sisters," I say. "I used to look up to them. You have it wrong. They hate me."

"That is not true," she says. "Keira says you told her mean things about her and Kali. You should not treat your sister so. They love you."

My sisters love me? I could almost laugh. "Well they have a funny way of showing it. They say mean things to me."

"Perhaps that is true. But they love you. Maybe you should show them some kindness sometime."

"Show them kindness? How could you say that to me when you know nothing on how I grew up? How they treated me? How everybody treats me, still."

She looks disturbed and sighs. "We do not hate you. We pretend to hate what the shaman thinks is inside of you, but we do not hate you." She stands and comes closer to me as I squat back over my rocks. Her knees are inches away from brushing mine as she squats next to me. She looks at the other women in the hut and frowns. "You have business, attend to it. Quit your eavesdropping!" A few of the women unabashedly turn away, smiles on their faces.

"We don't hate you," Okalaki says again. "We have been

taught to hate what is inside of you. This wickedness that the people have been led to believe about you. Not every woman knows the truth about you but many of us do and we are always talking about you in the women circles. You should have joined us. You would have learned lots."

"How can I join something when I am so unwanted? I am pushed away so I go and be somewhere I am wanted."

"In the forest?"

"Where else? Women are afraid to go into the forest—but not me!"

"We are not afraid, we are wary—there is a danger that lurks there, a danger you do not understand."

"Yeah—I know of it. The black panther. The very thing everyone thinks is my spirit animal. The one that stalks me. I know."

Okalaki frowns and then shakes her head. "That is not it. That is not why we fear the forest."

I stop and hesitate, choosing my next words carefully. "What do you mean, not what you fear? If not the black panther, then what?"

Her voice is low and for my ears alone. "There is another monster in these woods—a claimed beast unlike the black panther."

"What is it?" I ask, suspiciously. I have never seen any other creatures in the woods. Rarely have I ever seen the black panther and I can count the encounters on my hands alone—but not this other creature. What could be feared more than the black panther?

"A black snake," Okalaki says. "It hurts."

This is the first time I have ever heard of this black snake. "What does it hunt?"

"The black panther." Okalaki says grimly. "And you."

"Black Panther? Me?" I shake my head and laugh. "Why would it be after me? Another story to tag along with my name of being wicked. A witch. Spirit walker. Enticer of evil spirits!"

"Knock it off, Ara Macao and listen to me!" The fierceness in her voice has me closing my mouth and leaning away from her. "That is better. Now listen, you need to be careful. I do not know what is going on with the shaman and these traders, but something is not right. Something is amiss. Surely, you can sense it?"

I narrow my eyes at her. "I might have. But I am a witch. I am a spirit walker, remember? I have these odd quirks about myself that make me not right. Of course, I sense wrongness from these strangers. I sense a wrongness from the shaman. I even sense it about you, too!"

Okalaki sighs and leans against the hut. "It is sad that you think how you do, though, I understand it. Too much isolation, too much time alone with the forest walker. Yes—I know if him. Though I know him differently than you do."

"You—you know him?"

"It is not my secret to tell," Okalaki says, closing her eyes and then she opens them and looks right at me again. "We need to get you out of this arrangement. This pairing."

"What?" I blink at her. That did not make any sense. This is what my people wanted. And I say as much to her.

"No, it is a ruse. It is what we want the men to think. For the shaman to think. Your father has not been acting himself lately. He has been spending too much time with the Shaman."

"They have always been close," I say.

"Yes," Okalaki agrees. "But he is different. Even Menoa, your mother, has commented on it. Your grandmother is nervous for what may come. The shaman is up to something. Ara Macao, you must find a way to get out of the agreement with the traders and flee. You need to find your black panther—the spirit animal that has been stalking you—and claim him." She reaches over and takes my hands, while her eyes glance furtively at the others for eavesdropping. When she was satisfied she looks back into my eyes. I blink with surprise. Surprised at the touch, surprise at the familiarity she touches me. I am too shocked to move. "You must complete the bond with the spirit animal and become a spirit walker. You must unlock your hidden magic. You must find the source of the strangeness—this evil—and destroy it.

I try to pull away from her. "I don't understand what you are talking about. Have you lost your mind, Okalaki? Is it too hot in here? Are you thirsty?"

"Remember these words! You must complete the bond and find the source of the evil. Nobody has told you the truth for fear of attracting the shaman's notice. You must find out the truth. You are the only one of us left. You are the last of us!"

"The last of… us?"

"Of the people. Of the Spirit Walkers."

I scoff. "Spirit walkers are evil beings that bond with animals and have magic. Witches. Spirit walkers." I shake my head, my hair swaying with the movement. "What you are saying is crazy."

"No," Okalaki says with a shake, pulling my hands and inadvertently shaking me. "Spirit Walkers is an ancient power women have. Only women. Men are hunters. Women are the true healers alongside our spirit guides. But we do not have them anymore."

"Have what?"

"Our spirit animals. They have been stolen from us. And I have come to learn—perhaps too late—that the shaman is doing more than what he claims."

"What are you talking about?" Spirit animals were things of men. Women did not have them. It is why I am considered so wicked because it is said that I have an unbonded spirit animal. That I use his powers for my evil. It is why the shaman has watched me so closely all of my life and has let me loose in the woods, alone, because he wishes me to die.

"The shaman takes them from us when he learns that a woman has one. You are the last one. Bond with the panther. Become a Spirit Walker before it's too late." She brushes her hair from her face, it has come down around her face messily. "I have a plan to get you out of this. You will escape into the night. I will provide a distraction for you.

I want to laugh in her face. She was spouting nonsense to me. My sisters love me? Spirit Walkers are good? Women have had spirit animals? Magic? It is too much.

My sister have treated me with disdain and have ruined my reputation since I was a child. The villagers hated me. The feared me. They thought evil things of me. Even my own parents dislike me. My mom fears what I will do next in case it shames the family and my father wants to beat me into submission. And now, someone who has always treated me with indifference says I have magic, that I have a spirit animal and am the last spirit walker? It is just too much.

Okalaki sighs. "I see that you do not believe me. Your grandmother wanted to be the one to talk to you."

Her words spurned a memory, the river, grandmama with her feet in the water. She had said something similar…

"Your sisters have not always been nice, and the people of the village have not treated you well. We will make a change of that. Starting tonight. You'll see." This time I do laugh and shake my head at her.

Heads jerk up in fright as a roar sounds out. It does not sound too far away.

It comes again, nearer.

I meet Okalaki's eyes. "Time to get you out."

WOMEN HUNCHING TOGETHER, STAND FROM THEIR SQUAT, stopping the turning of their blood rocks. Distant shouts were heard in the night. Strange men shouting orders. Screams were heard.

"It comes! It comes!"

"Demon in the forest—it has finally come!"

"Big, so big! Its fangs are so large!"

"It wrestles with the black panther!"

"The shaman? Where is the shaman?"

More shouting and running feet goes past the wigwam. And then silence. Whatever is going on, is happening right outside the village. One thing Okalaki said was right, I needed to leave. I need to leave this place and quickly while the villagers are distracted.

"What do you think is going on out there?"

"I think I heard the Black Panther roar," another says.

"We all did," someone sounds annoyed. "What is it fighting?"

Eyes fall onto me and my hands ball into fists at my waist. "Why do you all look at me? I have done nothing."

"She is right," Okalaki says, stepping in front of me. My eyes widen at the gesture. "She has done no wrong."

"Then who has caused this if not her?" a woman asks. She is new to the village and already she thought ill of me.

"She has been with us the entire time," Okalaki says, hands on her fists. "Three hot days, she has been here with me. She has done nothing. Whatever is happening is not of her doing." Though she does not glance at me, I can tell that she was nervous.

"Then whose spirit animal attacks us?"

"You women have been fed lies. All of it is lies. This is not the work of Ara Macao or any spirit animal. This is the work of something else."

"What do we do?"

"Do?" Someone says hesitantly. "What can we do, we are not done with the purification process?"

"We can do nothing," Okalaki says. "We have to wait this out. Allow our hunters and warriors to handle this. Our husbands are out there they will protect our children and our families and our friends. But we can go and hide. We will be safe."

"Aren't we better safe inside here?"

"Surrounded by blood?" Okalaki asks back at them.

"The shaman," someone says. "He will cast the evil spirit out. I saw him with the spirit catcher. He has his black staff, and he is catching spirits."

"Spirit catcher?" I ask. That was a word I had never heard before.

"The spirit catcher," Okalaki says, grimly. "Is his staff with holy rocks and ancestral feathers meshed together at the end. Though I do not understand what it does. It should not be able to do the things that he has it do."

"But what does it do?"

Okalaki stares at me as if I am an idiot. "It wards off spirits. It chases them away. Just being in the vicinity of the holy object can make the spirits go away and prevents them from harming the living. The shaman can vanquish them, but he cannot capture them with it. It is ill named."

"That is not true," a woman says. "I have seen him absorb the spirit animal. I have! He came to our village once, to dispel an evil spirit. Instead of vanishing—it—it, was absorbed!"

Okalaki looked ill at ease. Something in those words upset her, but what? More shouting in the distance. Shouts for the shaman to come. Where was Zakopelli?

I feel a hand on my arm and look up to see Okalaki staring me in the eye. "If they capture the shadow cat, it is all over. Please, trust me in this. I do not know what is going on out there, but please, trust me. try to trust me. I know we have never given you a reason to trust but please, I ask this of you, trust me. We need to distract them, to prevent the shadow cat's capture at all cost. It will be the beginning of the end for all of us if he is capture."

Things on the outside seemed to quiet. In fact, they seemed to quiet. Where had all the shouting voices gone to? *Where were the screams?*

Abruptly, the door to the hut burst open, I duck as shards of woven grasses and wood flies' inwards, falling onto the fire, casting us into darkness. A dark figure looms over the threshold. I can see the green predator eyes of the spirit walker. They flashed the cat glow as they fall onto me. I sniff the air, cool evening air comes into the shack, and something else, something familiar. A musky, earthy smell.

"Not in here! Go spirit, run! Now is your chance, Ara Macao. Go!"

Okalaki charges the spirit animal and as the black panther raises his claws to strike the birthing woman down, and my voice erupts into the darkness, "No!"

The panther looks at me, hesitating just a moment before Okalaki slams into it. The cat gets up and runs, fleeing from her.

Okalaki does not seem to take glory with her accomplishment at scaring the spirit animal away, she turns to the rest of us. "Come on women let's get out of here! It is searching for something that we must leave, or we will die." Then she turns to me. "You know what you need to do, do it!"

"But we are in the process of purification," one of the women says. I can tell it was from an outsider. Nobody argues with Okalaki. Not the birthing woman. The midwife. When she says, hop, you hopped.

"Dammit woman," Okalaki yells. "Either stay here and die or come and run and hide. We saw the panther, but what about the snake?"

"Snake?" Someone cries out.

That got them going. As if with a single mind, the women surge forward, past Okalaki, and out into the village. Okalaki just a breath behind. I smell smoke on the wind and hear crackling flames behind me as the fire surges to new life with the added fodder. I do not follow Okalaki, I turn in the opposite direction. The direction that the panther had run.

If she wants me to capture this cat and keep it alive—then why did she just scare it away?

Nothing is making any sense.

As my feet move and I flee from the wigwam, I thought I saw Okalaki take up a torch and charge towards the forest alone.

Then I saw a familiar bow and quiver of arrows. I did not question what fate had aligned with me as I passed the shabono. Thank you ancestor.

It is the bow and quiver that had been taken from my father, the ones crafted by Banu. They are special to me.

My time in the hut is over, the flow between my legs had ebbed—if not dried completely, and I was ready to face the world. To face my silent stalker that has tormented me my entire life.

A spirit animal that wants me, a woman, to bond with. Well —I will do as Okalaki says but only in part. I will find this demon cat and I will be the one to destroy it, despite my grandmama's fears. I knew that only I could do this and in doing it I could finally become part of the village. If that did not work out—I could be with Banu. Always, with him I have a place. And why not both? Maybe if I destroyed this evil spirit, I could have Banu in the village with me and the people would accept me for who I am.

Whatever I chose, Banu or the man my people wanted me to pair with, I had a spirit to vanquish. And I am determined to do it before the shaman has the chance to do it.

18

______

Crouching along the wall of the shabono, I wait. Listening to sounds of the village, and the quiet air of the jungle.

Screet. Screet. Screet.

Something was making a scratching sound not too far away, out in the darkness of night. The village is immersed into shadow, only a couple standing torches around the center of the village gave any light, and they too, were dimming. A mist seemed to be descending upon the village.

The ground smells of wetness, a blend of fragrances—and most of all, I no longer smell the stench of sweaty bodies or heat rocks. Yet… there was another scent I tasted on the wind. A familiar musk. The scent of fear.

Something was about to die.

Within my chest, my heart beat rapidly against my body and it was hard to keep my breathing quiet. How does one force a bond with a spirit animal?

It was something of men—something I could not understand. How could Okalaki expect me to do this?

But I am not going to bond an evil animal. I am a woman. I have been judged wrong all of my life. Tonight, it ends. Tonight, I kill the demon!

Thump. Thump. Thump.

My breath came out in small puffs of air in front of me. Where are all the people? The village feels abandoned. As I pass a family home and make my way towards the outside, I peek inside the opened doorways to find bodies. Lots of bodies lying where they have slept. My heart give a lurch.

I sniff the air.

No! It cannot be. It cannot!

They smell warm. And then I sense their hearts beating in their bodies. The soft sigh of their breath coming from their nose as they sleep.

Puzzled. I do not understand this. Could they still be asleep?

My heart beats a little gentler, but something is wrong. I know it in my body and in the soles of my feet.

This is all wrong.

Why do they sleep?

I leave the shabono and find a body not too far away. A village woman—someone I recognized. The woman lies on her face, one leg up against her bell as the other is stretched out. Dropped as if she had been running. My hand descended upon her cheek and I can see that she is still breathing. I brush aside some of her hair. It is Zachi.

"What happened Zachi?" Though I knew that she would not answer. She was a deep sort of sleep. A trance.

In the village I hear a sound and I do not know what pulls

me, but my feet turn, and I run towards that sound, my bow and an arrow ready to notch in my hands. Wind blows from behind, pushing me forward toward something unknown. I lift my nose towards the mist, hoping for a little breeze to catch the scent danger.

This is why I am alive. This is what I live for. The hunt.

I enjoy hunting at night. It was a time when eyes did not matter; only my feet and hands, my ears and nose were the tools I need to find success.

Danger.

Instantly, I become alert, the last stretches of my moon flowering long forgotten. There is a scent that I recognize. I inch to the edge of the village, the dark jungle looms like a wall of shadow behind the fog.

I look back, towards the dim orange glow that bounces off the walls of the shabonos behind me. All the people... were asleep? I can see bodies now, where I stand at the edge of the village. There were more than just Zachi on the ground. Others. Here. There. As if fallen where they had run.

I stare back into the looming shadow of the trees.

I crouch and wait.

***

WHERE HAVE ALL THE PEOPLE GONE? THE WARRIORS WHO SHOULD have been alert and watching. The women who stay up all night with the babies. The wandering grandmother or grandfather who seem to be searching for something in the night.

And what has happened to those who lie on the ground as if falling asleep?

There is a rustle, a stirring in the trees, a wind moving through. My skin pricks with bumps as I see the mist beginning to clear.

I grow uneasy. Nervously, I run my fingers along the bow, while still holding onto an arrow. This would be my only protection tonight.

I train to hear and now not even the wind is blowing her soft sighs. It is absolutely silent. Deep and total. It is unnatural.

Growing alarm fills me, and I give myself room to draw back the fletching of the arrow for when it flies. I adjust my arms. Preparing myself for the moment it is loosed. I would only have one shot. If the demon came for me, if I see lurking, I will make that one-shot count.

The hoot of an owl sounds in the village, long and low. Terror boils in my stomach.

It is the cry of the harbinger of death!

Death is coming.

I crouch low. The cold night wind comes again with the taste of rain. Or maybe that was just a mist. All I have to do is wait.

A coldness splatters against my skin. Drop of ice hit my head and my arms and slide down my body like tears brought on from the sky. Raindrops, falling few at first before it came down consistently. I listen with relief. It is the heat season when SunFather's glory shines the brightest—perhaps the rains will come early this year—preventing long drought. If it rained, that would be advantageous for my people this night for the predator's dislike to hunt when it rains.

My arm aches and my stomach reminds me that I have had very little to eat in the last few years. I feel weak from hunger, I hope this would not drag out throughout the night. Cold seeps up from the ground and my fingers grow numb. The purification process, women who were not experiencing the monthly flowering visit the woman huts to make sure there is food and that they have water. I have had to survive off of the bear offerings of what others did not want to have to eat. Thus, I have survived the last few days.

My thoughts return to Banu. Over the last few days it is all I can do to keep myself from going insane. I hope he is well right now and I know that he is probably frightened of my being around many people—I, too, have difficulty with being around too many. I feel agitated. I feel confined.

Stop it! Focus on the hunt. Focus.

I was not one to be distracted when on the hunt.

Stop it. Focus.

There are shouts in the distance. I strain my ears to listen, cocking my head to the side to catch the sound. They sounded excited.

The hairs on my back and neck stand on end as I hear a voice in my head. "Go and see, child. Go and find out before it is too late." The voice sounds like that of my grandmama.

Click. Click. Click.

A familiar black staff hitting the ground with each step of his stride. I tense as I know who this man is. Who is coming? I duck down, behind a pile of hatch and timber as a light shines through the rising mist, swirling purple and white glowing with menace; Zakopelli strides past me. Red and Blue macaw feathers dancing a jig with each strike of the staff on the ground.

What was this old man doing? What could the shaman do this night? What was it that Okalaki has said? This was the man who keeps spirits away by stealing them. If a spirit is nearby, he could sense it too.

That also means…

That my father will also be there. He and the shaman were inseparable. Wherever one went the other would appear.

I stand briskly, my feet following after the shaman. I do not want to be seen, not yet, I knew my reputation and people will not think it wise or good to see me here if they have caught the beast before I could do the job.

Discreetly I follow behind the shaman, his feet smacking the ground like a large deer's hooves on stone, mine making soft wisps as I place the balls of my feet on the ground—hunting the man.

"Zakopelli," I hear the voice of Aba's mate. It is Tuonko. "We have found the beast. The snake has it cornered after it tried to flee."

"She caught the cat?" Zakopelli flicks the medallion at his neck and it is the first time I have noticed it. It is the source of the light. "I will reward her for her efforts."

From near the trees there are shouts, cries of joy and even noise some laughter. Whatever has happened word has spread far faster he has to me. The shaman holds up his finger as Tuonko looks to be on the verge of speaking.

"Silence, Tuonko."

"We got it! We got it!"

"Village leader has got the beast by the throat!"

"The Jaguar meets the panther in battle. Come, all men are needed to suppress its dark magic!"

Bodies run past me, people who I had not even seen, zip past me out into the night. I see that they are the bodies of those who were lying prone. More of the warriors. The hunters. Only men.

"Come on, men! Together, now!"

More bodies run past me, clad in strange cloth and materials and I recognize that they are the foreigners. They want to witness the events that are about to unfold. I find that my legs are running, too. I run past the shaman who looked at me with wide eyes as I fly past him with the power of the panther in my speed.

Clink. Clink. Clink. The staff hitting the ground as the shaman now pursuits me—to the hill side where the events are taking place.

There are people forming a circle near the forest edge I can see them lit up by the moonlight shining through the broken clouds above. The mist dissipates, the rain stops. The wind pushes the clouds apart to allow the rays of the MotherMoon to shine down to be witness to this judgment.

"Do you see it?" The Shaman says coming up from behind me. "You're about to be one of the few women to witness a spirit animal be overpowered by the strength of a man. That man already holds a spirit animal, if he captures that one, I say it will die."

I do not take my eyes away from the scene that is playing out. "Ah," I say aloud. That would make sense. Spirit animals are a thing of men, no woman has ever witnessed the bonding between man and beast. Disable the creature. Hold on to it until the shaman makes his timely arrival. Dozens of eyes are on the pair at the center of the circle. This was not just any beast or any spirit, it was the spirit animal of the black panther.

"I would not watch this, if I were you, Ara Macao. Go back to the huts." I had this urge inside of me to do just that, to do as he says, immediately. It took all of my might and will to ignore it.

The shaman passes me as I stand still and watch from the hill overlooking the gathering people. I have never been witness to the events of when hunters capture a spirit animal and clean them of their wills.

I have imagined it was with arrows and spears, and a great chase, or perhaps a fight with claws out, teeth bared, with a hunting knife flashing, slicing and cutting. But something tells me that this is the way; of overpowering, the forced submission.

And then death.

Where the animal serves the person as a bonded spirit animal.

A proceeding I thought that would be silent, respectful, was met with hollers, shouts, and jeers of laughter. The men clapped and stomped their feet. Spears hit the ground in a rhythmic tune as if in a trance.

In the circle, I see a large, tough looking man with wide shoulders, with the strength of ten men. His arms are crossed with judgement. It is my father… he stands watching as another man fights the panther.

His arms bulge with power, his muscles flexing with his iron grip on the beast the forest. I recognize him. It is the foreigner who is supposed to be my mate on the morrow and held my stalker. The demon of the forest.

As the shaman approaches, the circle of people part as if a round stone in water. The holy rocks glisten in MoonMothers light. Red and Blue feathers danced with iridescence at the moment of judgment pulls the one who carries the staff to the scene.

Green eyes of the panther look up. At first I thought they looked at the shaman and the symbol for which the holy man represents but then I realize, that they were not looking at the shaman. Green eyes, similar green eyes like mine are staring back at me. My heart lurches.

Banu!

The wood is strong in my hands, I feel it flexing in my grip. The string is made of roughly woven fibers from animal gut, and I feel it thrum in my fingers as I pull the arrow to my cheek; the fletching tickles my cheek and I hear the sweet tang as it is loosed.

In a breath's moment, I react. I move. Reaction causes action. Nothing can save me now.

The arrow hits the target right in the side of the head. Collectively, the hunters and the tradesmen react as one, falling silent, their movement ceases as shock fills their hearts almost as much as it fills my own.

Tears fall from my eyes as the people of my tribe and those of the water turn and stare back at me.

The shaman, Zakopelli, turns and looks in my direction, a frown etching his old withered face as he seems surprised that I still linger on that hill.

He raises his staff towards me, the crystals and feathers dancing over his head like protective spirits. "Betrayer of people! Spirit walker! Get the spirit walker!"

I stand there, dumbfounded at what I have done. Tears continue to fall from my eyes as many people surge forward to grab me. And I stand there, unmoving and allow the assault to come.

My father is the first of them, running on powerful legs. His dark, cold eyes, unfamiliar eyes, stare back into mine as his fist meets the side of my head.

Not far away, I thought I saw Okalaki standing near my grandmama, who is holding my mama.

They are weeping.

A strange thought passes through my mind before I meet darkness; who are they weeping for, surely not me?

19

Eyes peer at me through the cracks of my isolation. It was one of the shabonos that has been recently constructed. I can't help but wonder if they will bring it down in fear my being in here will be the only time it will be used… when those of the wicked are placed in isolation, it is believed that the evil essence of those within leech off and attach their damnation to the walls.

Fire and smoke would be used to cleanse this ground.

I stare back at the eye that peers at me through the hole in the thatch. It blinks and disappears but not before it reappears. I hear giggling. And I realize the eye belongs to that of a child.

Well—that is nice. I am being watched by little children.

I bare my teeth at the eye and growl, showing all of my teeth in a rictus of a snarl. More giggles ensue.

"Get out of here! Go away!" A familiar voice says.

The children erupt with laughter and disappears from the

hole as the place grows dark with a body. Then another eye appears.

"Ara Macao? It is me, Okalaki. Why did you not run?"

"I tried to save the spirit—well—kill it."

"Kill? You fool. You missed completely. Do you know who you have killed?"

"Yes," I say solemnly. "I know who my arrow has hit."

"So, you do realize the consequences to it? They are asking for your death."

"I—of course!"

"You tried to kill the… you are a fool. Look, I have an idea to get you out of this. Leave it to me. I will try to help. Your grandmother and mother will risk their lives with this plan. Got to go now, please, be steadfast!"

"Wait!" I call out as Okalaki, but she already ran off. Steadfast she says as if I have anywhere else to go. I sat, in isolation. As a prisoner. My back presses against the firm wooden poll that is at the center of the hut. I wish I could have told her that I attempted to rescue the spirit animal after it reminded me of a friend…

I can hear weeping in the distance, voice soft and somber. Frightened. They sound scared as though they have been attacked by the panther or have been caught up in the conflict of the previous night.

The village had been asleep when the attack had happened. Everyone but the men and the few women in the wigwam had been asleep.

During a time of conflict, I imagine the women coming together, embracing one another, unified in their confusion, fright and hatred of what has happened. An evil spirit so close to the village—in the village and a death occurring in the same night.

Alone in my hut, I have never felt so low. I, the outcast. An outcast like Banu. I could never learn where he has come from, but he has always been there.

My nose crinkles at the smell in the air. Smoke. I can smell smoke in the air wafting through the cracks of the hut. Ordinarily these huts are well constructed. A barrier to the outside world. This one has been hastily done for me.

The hunters have me locked in here. They block the exits to my escape. I have no chance of escape. And I will face my punishment for the crime I have committed. No longer does my father's hand seem so scary. The flames crackling outside frightens me now.

It is well known what happens to those who commit evil such as I have done. No longer can anyone excuse my behaviors on youth. Banishment would not be a fitting punishment for one such as I.

To kill a spirit walker...

...A need for flame and smoke were required.

And only then will the evil spirit of the person and their beast be vanquished.

It has happened before, stories of such an occasion would be retold at our campfires at night. Such things happened in other villages because ours did not have wicked women.

Except me.

For I am wicked.

And I am that evil.

Black glossy strands of hair touch the ground around my feet as I hang my head over my knees. I cannot help for who I am. My quirks, my differences, they were who I have been since I was little. Rock twirling, avoiding eye contact, fidgeting, digging, tree climbing, swinging and even my outbursts. People get under my skin easily and like the colorful parrot I have been named after to keep me holy, I screech, and I fly where I please. Despite my circumstances, my fingers still rove the ground for a pebble.

There would be none here for the shaman made this area out of sand from the river bottom. All the rocks and pebbles had been removed. It would have been comfortable place to rest if it were not my cage. I need not glance up at the little feathers and white rocks hung from cords from the ceiling. Precautionary charms to keep my evil from leeching off of those around me.

No longer could youth hide me from what was to come. I have done a great wrong, openly, and many sees my deed. My terrible act.

I had killed last night. I hope my friend will forgive me. For I will not be returning to him in the woods. I can never be able to talk to him about the things I have learned.

Wallowing in pity, for the first time in my life, I finally understood. I knew something about Banu that he has never told me before. Throughout my life, I have been stalked by the spirit walker; the Black Panther from the woods.

How stupid am I for not realizing it sooner? The forest boy. Banu. Why did he never tell me his truth?

Tears fell from my cheeks, dripping onto my dirty feet and making small grey spots in the sand. I breathe through my mouth for my nose was clogged. I had struck down someone to save the life of someone I am in love with. To save the person, I love, I had killed the tradesmen leader. The one who I would be paired with.

Finally, a truth of evil against my name. I had not killed that man long ago when I was a child.… But I did kill one last night.

Angry shouts echoed in the village. My father and the shaman were probably still trying to cool the heat from the traders. Nico, the leader of the traders, had a son with him, and I have heard his voice above the others, screaming for the witch to be brought forward.

To throw me tied onto the fire. *To burn.* But most of all, he wanted to hurt me before I face my punishment. I understand his feelings. If someone would have killed someone that I love, I would feel the same. In fact, I feel the same against myself right now. I wanted to throw myself onto that fire, not for pious reasons either. But for the guilt I felt after loosing the arrow. Before it had killed the traders, it had flown through my friend's arm and into the tradesmen's head.

I do not think my people even cared that I had loosed an arrow. Or that I have been in the same vicinity as the shadow walker. They were angry not because I had killed a man but because I had killed someone I was to be paired with. They want to be rid of me, and I have ruined that chance.

No death awaited me. Their only chance to be rid of me now.

And I am nothing without my Banu. I have cried out all of my tears, nothing more would be coming. The last tear drops from my chin and I close my sore eyes in shame.

It is bad that I have no remorse for it is probably made even worse for I hurt and regret having hurt my friend. An injury that I will never forgive myself in. I can only hope that he will be well—and if he is indeed the spirit animal—that he takes me to the fathomless void in my death where I will be alone and shunned for all eternity.

I hear voices outside that do not conceal themselves. The shaman is making preparations.

"We must. She is a wayward spirit."

"She is my granddaughter! You cannot take her."

"Your granddaughter but you know as we as I, with her gone the village will be at peace. The wickedness will be gone. My wife might even bear a son for me!" The voice of my father cuts me.

"Your wife has three beautiful daughters!"

"Don't count your feathers before they are pulled," someone says.

"Maybe," someone else adds. A familiar voice. One of my sisters? "We should just let her go. You saw her. I saw her, my sister Keira saw her too. She had tried to shoot the Black Panther. She tried to make it go away. She did not mean to kill the man."

Jumbled voices broke out. They were arguing again, and I cannot make out everything that is being said. Voices were overriding each other until they became a blurred cacophony that pantomimed the raucous macaws of my name sake. Just noise. All I hear is noise. I shudder at the commotion—my senses tell me to flee.

My arms tremble with emotion at being kept in what feels like a cage, with loud voices screaming all around me. There are walls to my cage—the hut is a pentagon of woven materials and the ceiling roughly construed so that the sunlight fell in rays of light.

"That does not matter. The spirit will not die just because the girl does. The shaman needs to dispel it. Only the shaman can do this."

"She disrupted the chance for the shaman to do this. This is her punishment."

"D—Death... f-for an a-accident?" My mama says between gasps, she sounds like she is hyperventilating, and I realize that she is crying. Still, after a long night, she cries for me. My heart wants to break inside my chest. "Do accidents now re-require somebody to die?"

"Her arrow flew through the creature and into the man. No way did she know that would happen." The voice of another woman speaks up. It is Okalaki. "She was only trying to do some good. And if you all would use your brains instead of your emotions, you would see that."

"That does not matter," a man speaks up, guttural and unused to speaking the language of the people. It sounded bitter. "My father is dead. Yes—yes I do speak the language of your people though it sours my tongue to do so. Justice must be had for the world to be right. I demand this. Shaman Zakopelli, I demand it of you. We have what you want. You failed my father, but will you fail me too? Are you going to insult me further?"

"What do you mean?" Okalaki demands. "What does he mean, Zakopelli? What do they have that you want?"

"Calm down, Menoakiki," the shaman says placating. "He

only means trade. Don't you son?" The surrounding sand stirred a little, dust rose into the air with his words.

"Yes, trade. Of course, that is what I mean."

"You see? He threatens us with no trade. That means no prosperity for our village. We have many people who have come to the village the last few days, how are we to care for them all? He offers us not only chests of clothing and supplies like knives—things we cannot make on our own—for the girl's life. Justice. His father's dowry, a gift for being paired. This would help us greatly Menoakiki."

"You would kill a young girl for treasure? We have many strong men in our village—they will hunt good for the people as they have always had."

My mother's voice chimes in hopeful, "and if you raise the barring on fishing, the women can support the village with foods from the river."

"Silence!" Zakopelli shouts. "Women be silent." More dust rises into the air.

"They do not see what you are doing, Zakopelli, but I can!" My grandmother spat. "You are changing, Zakopelli. What is becoming of you?"

"Nothing has become of me, woman. I am and have always been, Zakopelli, shaman. Take this old one away—it would seem her wits are not about her this day. Sad day for the old."

"Unhand me you fools. I am completely sane. Don't you all see what is happening, what the shaman is doing? Don't you see." Grandmama's protests continued until they became too hard to hear over the rush of voices.

"But my daughter," my mama began again but is suddenly hushed.

A sneeze wells up from me, not once but twice and thrice more before I am coughing. I shield my mouth with my hand, trying to prevent the dust from coming into my body. It does little to help. I cover my face with both of my hands and breathing through my teeth.

A monotone voice speaks up and I realize it is Pia speaking. She does not sound the same, though always soft spoke, her voice sounds off. "We need to consider everything. She was to be paired. She killed the one she was to be paired with. She killed the one who would have made her behave. There is need of justice. This is justice."

"Nicely put, Pia," the shaman said smoothly.

"It does not matter if she tries to do good, her actions killed a man," a man's voice says. Usually strong and heated in his desire to be heard. It is Tuonko, second to Caboko. Aba's mate. His voice, too, sounds strange. Monotone and without inflection. "She killed the leader of the traders. Either we kill our village leader who has always protected this village, or, we choose the one who has committed the crime and punish her justly."

"This is not right," Tosha says. "Pia why would you say this?"

"It is the right thing to do," Pia respond.

"An eye for an eye, eh?" Okalaki says. "That has never been like you. You were one to always stand up for Ara Macao's strangeness. Why do you change your tune so suddenly, girl?"

"It is the right thing to do," Pia says again.

"You people want to stand in the way of justice?" The shaman asks angrily. "And what about our friends of the water?"

"We will do something to make it right," Tosha says firmly. "Not with Ara Macao's death."

I can just see Okalaki with her thick hands on her hips as she nods with agreement. "We will trade something they always want. The rocks from the rivers and mountains streams."

The shaman scoffs. "The men will be busy hunting to feed the many mouths—they do not have time to look for the holy rocks!"

Aba chimes in. "I have gotten better at fishing—I can fish."

A chuckle sounds nearby. "Only if you do not eat it all for yourself." It is Zosha. "Ouch—no need to be violent sister."

"Quiet, Zosha, this is no time for jests. A girl's life is on the line," Zachi says. "I, too, can fish. We all can."

"And who says the men need to do all the searching for the holy rocks? We can all help. We can teach the new women how to do this. Surely a trade in holy rocks of white diamonds will make these traders happy. Will it make you happy?" Her question was not addressing Zakopelli but the young trader who has just lost his father.

"I—I..." The dust thickens and I cannot stop it from getting into my mouth and up my nose and into my lungs. I begin coughing again. My eyes are squeeze shut with the agony at trying to breathe.

"The girl does not sound well—she must be sick. Sick of mind and of body," The shaman declares.

"But you cannot rule what these tradesmen will trade. Diamonds. He wants diamonds for trade. Leave the girl alone. She is unwell of mind and body. Leave her alone. Take the treasures we can supply you."

The shaman begins to splutter as some mutual sounds of

agreement came from the traders as the boy relayed the conversation to his peers.

"And why can we, women, not hunt for these rocks? Hunt for fish? Why only the men?"

"Zakopelli has many secrets," my mama says suddenly, her backbone suddenly coming to life as the voices from the other women gather around. Mother was always a follower but in that moment my heart sighs with relief to hear her voice. "Menoakiki is right. You are hiding many things from us."

"Silence!" A roar fills my ears as I hear the staff striking the ground.

Astoundingly, there is silence. Complete silence.

And then the dust begins to settle.

"There will be retribution for the murder of their leader. Only smoke and fire can kill a spirit walker or the killing of her spirit animal. I, and only I, carry the staff that was made by our ancestors."

"What is your command?" Okalaki says. Her voice sounding monotone, without feeling.

"She must be killed on the pyre. Her screams will beckon her bonded spirit animal, and only then will we rid us of both evils at once."

The voices of the women and the gathered hunters are silent. Nobody raises derision or voices a difference of opinion. I can feel the trance suddenly lift, the buzz in the air that was not a buzz.

"She has had her moon flowering," Okalaki says. "The evil within her body has been vanquished. She is no longer what we had suspected her to be." My unlikely defender. She has always treated me with disdain. Looking down her large square face as if I am a bug to be stepped on. Maybe she had good intentions. Maybe she was never truly unkind to me but just a woman who saw me as ignorant and naïve. "What will we tell her grandmother?"

"Her grandmother is not the shaman or the village leader," Zakopelli says. "Your opinion has been noted. I am sure in the women's circle you are well in your station to speak. But here, I put my foot and my staff down and say enough. No more, Okalaki. You have said what you have said, and I have given the decision to be had."

"A hand for a hand. An eye for an eye. A life for a life." My father's voice speaks up. The voices no longer sounded deplete of emotion but instead resigned. "It is the way of these people from the waters, Okalaki."

"But father," Keira and Kali say together. "She is our sister. Please reconsider. As village leader only you have the right to make this decision. Not the shaman."

My heart lurches in my chest to hear the voices of my sisters speaking for me. It is the first time in my life that I hear them speak for me. And I sense the shaman beginning to grow angry.

"Father," Kali pleads. "Let her go. Banish her to the forest like when she was a child."

It is as if I could see my father crossing his arms with that austere face of his as he shakes his head. "I cannot allow that. She would only go back to the demon in the woods. I have tried, and I have failed to destroy that creature. She lays with it when no one is around to watch her. Commits evil acts in the woods. Hunts and behaves like a boy. Behaves like an animal."

"Then let us try to cure her again," Keira says. "We can make her behave like a girl. A woman. She needs to be around women to know how to act like them."

"She is too strange—not even I can make her change. If fists cannot do it, neither can a woman's touch."

"If it is the will of the village leader, then let us get this over with," Zakopelli says gravely.

"No father!" Keira and Kali say in unison. "Please father, don't do this."

"There is no cure for the incurable. She was born wicked and to death she will go wicked. Shaman, begin and let us be done with this. And finally," my father says, "my wife will be given another chance to have one more child. A son."

A soft cry is issued near the voice of my father. It is my mother weeping in her hands. I hear her sobs muffle as if someone was trying to soothe her.

"Aiko, I have not had my moon flowering in many years," my mama says between sobs. "I cannot bear you a son. Her death will not bring you a boy child."

"With Ara Macau out of the way. With the wicked out of this village. You will give me a son, or I will find a new mate!"

My mama cries. It is not the cry of losing a mate. But of losing a child. She knows as well as I do that father hates me because I had not been born a boy. With me out of the way perhaps he may have a son. Yet—I do not think so. It is not what the ancestors wanted for him and his greed and selfishness shrouds his thinking and has perverted his judgement.

"Shaman, get on with it."

"Yes, Aiko, a village leader of the cliffs."

I can see feet standing in front of the shack door. As the

door opens, SunFather's brilliance lights behind the being, so all I can see is a dark silhouette.

Death is coming.

Time to meet my punishment and what fate had in store for me.

20

The hairs from my body erect themselves like those from a thorny animal as Zakopelli stands as an ominous dark wall, watching as the hunters of my village tie my hands and my feet.

"This will be easier for you if you do not struggle," he says, grimly.

My father stands near him, arms folded across his large chest. "You will no longer shame us, daughter. Go with that knowledge."

They pulled me from the shack, I stumble and fall to the ground. The hunters, those eyes an angry red, do not care if I fall and if they have to drag me along until I am out in the open. I struggle to regain my feet as the cords pull tight and tug me along. They are careful not to touch me as I stumble again, my knees hitting the ground as I nearly collide into them, my skin becoming raw and scraped with their efforts.

Whispers erupt all around me. Whispers in the air. Whispers of dangerous secrets. Zakopelli walks at my side, a shroud of darkness seeming to pulse with each of his footsteps. I glance around to see if anyone saw what I did, but their eyes only held one person: me.

Yet my mind has only one thought. *What does my mama know about the shaman?* Surely she and my grandmama could see this darkness. Was it magic? His magic?

My grandmama and even Okalaki hinted that there was just one last spirit walker in this tribe, me. Who had been the others? I know that whispers of my grandmama holding a magic aura was said in hushed voices, but could it be true?

"Oh, look at her eyes—look how they glow green!"

My head snaps around and I am face to face with one of the strangers from the waters.

"She has the eyes of a panther," says another. I looked. It's a woman. Another person I do not recognize.

Who are all these people?

People from other villages and traders. But strangers in my heart.

"She has the eyes of the panthers."

"Keep her away from my children," a mother says as she ushers her kids behind her back. Another of the foreign women and her children from another village. She stares daggers down at me as if her stare can kill.

I feel it in my heart, the piercing glare from that woman. From all of them. I was loathed I was despised.

Yet. They could not hate me as much as I hated myself in that very moment.

The hunters did not slow as they drag me from my imprisonment. My fingers snag a rock as my knees hit the ground another time. It was as if I knew where exactly to find it. A little rock, unique that my mind had singled out in that frantic second to grab something. A round rock. I glance down at my fingers and see a white rock. A diamond. I could sense that it was special. The kind that I like to twirl around my fingers.

As they drag me after them, I could not help myself as my body began to vibrate. My arms tremble and fear builds up in me. My legs become rigid as if they do not know how to bend and I feel like I am hobbling along.

I am about to die.

My fingers pressed into the rock and I sigh with relief. The urge of twirling the rocks does not overcome me but a sense of peace comes emanates from the little stone. The little pebble between my fingers pinches and prods my skin and I close my eyes. I do not know why these little quirks of mine exist, but I am glad I am not overcome with the urge this time. Just holding the rock is enough.

"No twisting around a standing torch?" The shaman says as he looks at me. "There is a poll overhead, do you not have an urge to swing on it?"

"No," I say pointedly. "I do not feel the need to untwine myself."

He narrows his eyes at me but says nothing more.

"I wish you would have behaved like this before," my father whispers at me. "I have never seen you so well behaved."

My fingers flex against the stone and something inside of

me resounds like the cool river mud inside my blood. I do not feel goaded by his words.

The villagers accepted that I am about to die and allow me to walk in silence. The foreigners were not so thoughtful.

"Look at her look at her. What is it that she does that is so strange?"

"Strange things that are not of this world."

"One can never know the mind of a witch," the shaman says, gravely. "To understand a witch, you have to become one yourself. I advise against that. There is only one shaman here."

"Let us be done with this," my father says.

I am pulled to the center of the village, with two hunters in front of me holding the cords to my captivity. They stop and turn to face me and then they look at the shaman, then my father.

"Where are the tradesman leader's son? Does he not want here to observe her punishment?"

"The boy's father died last night; he is wrought with grief." One of the men, the sailors that is what he is called, "said that he may not make it. Ordinarily these trials are done in a court system. They take weeks to conduct. He feels that this girl who murdered his father is getting off too easily. He will not be here today."

"And where are the others?" my father asks.

"They, too, are gone. I am to stand watch to oversee that this deed is done. We can begin trades, tomorrow. Or the day after."

My father nods at him but see Caboko approach from outside of the village. "We may have trouble," the voice of Caboko says. I look over at him as he avoids my gaze. There is no reason for me to think that he may have sympathy for me, we have never been close. Out of all the hunters in the village, I have always liked Caboko. He seems to be the only one who does not look at me with disdain.

I admit it that there was a time that I might have fancied him, that was well before he decided to become mated with Tosha. He is very loyal to his mate, something to be admired, but he never treats me with disdain like the others. He sort of treats me with indifference for which I like about him.

"Caboko is right," my father says, leaning down to speak with the shaman. His eyes are on me, his mouth working into a frown. "No matter what I tried to do to punish the evil spirit, her nature only grew more and more dark. And now it will seem that she will make the villages be punished for her crimes." I cringe at his words but do not argue with him. It would be no use now.

"Not if we can help it," the shaman says. Zakopelli stares down at me, his face is pensive, and I dislike the look that he was giving me. A look of secrets, or ambition. He had always talked about trust and discernment during the night's campfires, and yet… there is something about him that I dislike. An aura that it seems that only I could sense. And I realize in this moment that I have mistrusted that man for a very long time.

My instinct says that I am correct, that I should not trust the shaman. Look at me now. My instincts have gotten me in this mess. My haste. My quirks. My irrational thinking. And now I face death.

"Ara Macau," the shaman says. I look up at him and his

mouth thins to a line. "Aiko, Caboko, give us space, won't you? I would like a few words with her alone."

"Yes shaman," my father says and turns and walks away. Caboko is a little more hesitant to leave. He gives me a furtive glance before he pantomimes my father and retreats.

"You do understand why we must do this, don't you?"

I close my eyes, squeezing them shut. And I nod my head. "Yes, I understand."

"Can you understand that we need your help just the same?"

Need my help? I open my eyes and glance back up at him. I think my mouth might have been hanging open because I shut it with a click. "You need my help?"

"You may not believe it, but we do not want to do this. I know it is hard to understand that, perceiving this situation from your end. Our hands have been forced. These are the causation of your actions. Actions have consequences, Ara Macao." His voice was soft, and it became even more tender as he continues to speak. "I have never thought to be the one to have to tell you this, but I think you are a remarkably special girl. The most special type of girl since your grandmother was a child. I have tried many times to protect you."

"Lies," I spat at him. "All of that is lies. I am only at fault for killing the trader. Everything else you say are lies."

"They are not lie, my dear. It is the truth. You look very much like your grandmother."

I absolutely did not. I am very tall whereas all the women in my family are short. I am lean whereas the women are curvy. My hair is thick and curly when not in many small braids, while there are gentle waves and straight strands.

"I can see that you doubt me. I can understand that. Know

that it is true and that from the time you were a little girl, I have protected you. Watched you. I, unlike anyone else in this village, understand you. Everything about you. You're unique. Different from the others."

"You have made my life hell since I was a child."

"I protected you."

"Some protection. You invoked hatred, undeserved hatred."

"I protected you," he says again, adamant in his beliefs. "The other women are tricksters; they hide things from me. I do my best to find out their secrets and yet they try to hide things from me. You, my dear, are open with your quirks. Your unique things that you do. You do not try to hide yourself from me. And yet you are very different from the others. You did not bond the spirit animal."

"I have no idea what you're talking about."

"No, you wouldn't because you are special." He reaches out and touches my cheek.

I pull away from him, careful not to stumble with the cords around my hands and my feet. "Special, special, special. Just shut up about that. And don't touch me."

"You know that we have to do this. It will not be easy. This is never an easy circumstance. I know you will have a difficult time saying yes, but I need your help."

"I would never help you in anything."

"You are the key to the dark spirit in the woods." He kneels besides me and brushes my hair back from my face. "Ara Macao, when the time is right, you will call forward your spirit animal. You must make him be in the form of a man."

"I do not have a spirit animal!"

"You don't, that is why you are so special. Unlike the others who try to hide their wickedness, you were never truly wicked. You are open. You never bonded a spirit animal. You walked a fine line of friendship with one. Which is the greatest bond of all?"

Banu? Does he mean Banu? My mind grew fuzzy with confusion and my fingers tensed around the white rock in my hand.

I shake my head at him. "I do not understand what you speak of." And yet, in part, I do. He was talking about Banu. But never in my life would I tell this man about Banu.

Zakopelli was quick of mind and sharper reflexes, his hand shot out and grabs mine and catching the little rock in his fingers. He holds the rock up curiously as eyes widen with surprise. "Remarkable. Where did you find this rock?"

"I don't know… I picked it up when I fell down." I shoot an accusing look at my father and then at the shaman and back into the hundreds behind them. Many people are gathered in the village square. A nervous tremble filled my limbs again. So many eyes were on me.

The shaman held out the tiny little rock in front of my eyes, the sun shining on it giving it a little white glow. "This is a holy rock," he says to me. "It's not the same as the white diamonds we give to the traders. It is plenty in this area and yet you have one, perfectly formed. You have bonded with this spirit animal, I think. Which makes you a spirit walker. The very first female spirit walker this village has seen in a very long time. You should not have been able to find a holy rock so casually, unless, the ancestors have permitted it. You see, this is a sign from our people in the sky."

"I do not understand," I say to him, shaking my head. "It is just a rock. My fingers like to find them and twirl them and play with them."

"And why do you think that is? Because the ancestors have bid you to do so. It is with this little rock that they want you to help us, the living people. They wish for you to think, to use the powers of a spirit walker to help us this day. Think about it. With your death and your help, you can do this one thing for the people. One selfless act can save everybody."

"Selfless act? What do you mean? Is it because I found a rock?" My head began to spin, and I know I was asking all the wrong questions.

The shaman only smiled kindly at me and I could see in his black eyes a burning ember growing in their depths. This was an evil man. "No because the ancestors gave you this rock during one of your special moments."

I can only shake my head at him, seeing that burning ember glow in his eyes frightened me. His hands on my skin frightened me.

He nods his head vigorously. "I have seen others do the things that you do. And they have always been spirit walkers. My wife was a spirit walker. A woman who dealt in the art of magic. But I see in you something I have never seen in the others. You have a goodness in your heart. It shows." He holds up the rock to my eyes, playing with it between his index finger and thumb before putting it back into my fingers holding my fingers into a fist. "This Little Rock is a gift from the ancestors, and it wants you, the last female spirit walker, to call forth the shadow cat..." His eyes burn into mine. They were no longer black, no longer brown or amber. They were the color of burnished copper that flash flames in the SunFather's light.

"When you breathe in the smoke, you must breathe in the magic of the holy rock. Only then will the shadow cat leave us alone. Only then will the people prosper. You can do this. Bring this cat forward as a man. Do it for the people. Have him try to save you from your fate."

"Do you even hear yourself? Why would I do this thing that you are asking of me?"

"You know who it is that you must bring forward. Bring forth the forest boy."

"And why would I ever do this thing that you ask of me? You treated me like a liar as a child. Got my people against me. Everyone hates me. Even now. Look at them and tell me that you did not plant these ideas of hatred in their hearts!"

"I can see why you would feel those things. But if you recall, I have never tried to harm your child. If you think hard, you can see the effort I tried to help you. We uplift each other for we are all the people. As for why you would want to do this thing, it is simple. When you die, your spirit animal will be out here in the forest along. He will try to bond with another. Do you want them to be bonded with another? To take another soul. With your death, you can bring him with you to our ancestors and both of you with this little rock in your hand can wash away your sins. That is why the ancestors gave you this rock. It is a chance for you to make things right. You were born special, not wrong, just special, but now you have a chance to be right. Help us be rid of the shadow cat in the woods. He has killed many, do not let him kill more."

"He would never kill anyone!" I do not believe the shaman. I could never believe such a terrible lie about Banu.

I have no reason to believe in him. He is the one who sent

me to banishment as a child. I could have died in these woods if not for Banu. He is the one who always told the people about the black panther being my spirit animal. It is he who tells everybody the lies about me, that they walk at night on all four legs. And when I first had my moon flowering, it was he who said that I was in heat and attracted the roars in the forest. It is he who had prevented myself from becoming a mate with any of men in the village, for fear that they could not claim me for I was too strong. Too powerful of a woman.

I glare at the shaman. Zakopelli.

He could tell by looking my face that I did not agree with them. He sighs and shakes his head at me.

Zakopelli stands and stares down his hawkish nose at me. "Tie her to the stakes. Let's get the fire burning. She will do this thing for us whether she likes it or not. Just wanted to give her the chance to do this last thing for the people with grace."

My father was all too eager to grab the first of the fire as his hunters pull me to the post at the center of the wood stakes. Tosha's mate stands nearby, he has not grabbed anything. He nods his head solemnly at me, his eyes full of sadness and something else, determination, before he turns and walks away.

My eyes glare at the crowd of villagers that have gathered around. The closest faces shock me. Tear stain faces stare back at me. Hopeless eyes, shamed. My sisters are in the front and they are clinging to each other crying. My mother is wailing. I do not see my grandmama. I don't think I will ever see her. Bless her for all that she has ever done for me. May she live many more seasons to come.

A pair of macaws, their brilliant red feathers, the colors of hot flames, flew across the sky, calling the raucous screech of their species. Something falls from the sky like a white tear drop and splashes on my face, dripping down to my chest, to the branches at my feet.

I have been laughed at this day and now even the ancestors shit on me.

21

Flames crackle and burn all around me. The dry tinder burns hot and the heat begins to feel uncomfortable. The fire burns with intensity and has not yet reached me. Villagers come up to the flames, carrying dry timber and grasses tied into thick knots.

I see them reach out, to let the fire lick its hot tongue at their bundles with its oranges dancing flames before they threw the fire lit tinder at me. A couple struck me on my leg and arms as I am unable to move out of the way. I nearly scream out in pain, the wind coming out of my lungs as a fierce hiss as the fire bites me and then blissfully, falls away, rolling on top of the hot wood.

Fear fills my heart. I begin to pant with it. I taste it driving up my body and to my mouth and nose.

Such great fear.

Children in the back are laughing or crying, playing with

their friends, while others stand near their parents and watch with somber eyes, reflecting the moods of their parents and the surrounding adults.

My father is standing near the front, his arms crossing in front of him, his usual stance of indifference. He is watching me with an intensity like nothing I have ever seen from him before. I tug at the bonds keeping me in place and something in his eyes stirs. Sympathy? Compassion? I would have laughed if it isn't such an absurd idea. But something in his eyes is moved at my plight, it is as if he wants to say something, do something that is out of character.

I sniff back the tears that threaten to come when my eyes do not see my mama or grandmama. They are nowhere to be seen. I hope they find comfort in the days to comes. My mama, I sometimes get the feeling that she is frustrated by me. That I do nothing right in her eyes. Deep down, I knew that she loves me. She just has a different way of showing it. The last few days I have observed her in a way I wish I had known. My mama has a backbone, it's just hides from all her insecurities cast by the shadow of my father.

Keira and Kali are present and it's the first time I have ever seen them with tears. Their faces are of shock. I am touched by their display if emotion on my behalf. I do not know if it's just a show they're putting up but their earlier words in my defense has cooled my anger towards them. What they have done to me, their torment of me, has not been resolved but a part of me has forgiven them. If only we had more time together.

Their friends stand nearby; Pia, Zosha, Tosha, Zachi, Aba, Tuli. All of them. They do not look happy. Somber eyes stare back into mine. Face blank or crunched up into a grimace, faces threatening to tear. Many look to wish to say something to me.

Tosha bit her bottom lip, her hand on her belly. Aba openly cries. Tuli and Pia look at me with red-rimmed eyes. Zachi and Zosha, so alike almost as near identical as my sisters, stare at me outrage. Maybe they all had regrets. Maybe it was a show. In that moment I do not feel alone. In that moment I feel that I have… friends. Friends of a delusional sort of feeling. I have never been close to any of these women but briefly, I feel that we could have been friends. Our differences set aside.

"Be strong, Ara Macao," Aba cries out.

"This is so wrong," Pia whispers, her words come into my ears above the crackling of the logs.

Someone throws wet grass onto the burning logs and smoke rises. The smoke stings my eyes, causing them to burn and water. I cough, and through my blurry vision I stare up at the sun and the blue sky, which was turning milky white for the smoke grew thick. Lightheadedness bogs my mind and I feel my head bounce onto my chest, I can no longer see the crowd of the villagers that have gathered around, my people, standing around the pyre. I know they stare back at me even if I cannot see them. They probably stood, watching, through the billows of smoke allowing visibility.

Through the haze, I see something white shining and little dark objects dancing around the glowing orb. The black staff was as clear as a shadow behind a wall of mist. A wall of smoke. It was the staff of Zakopelli. Vaguely, I can see a form standing near my father. Probably making sure that I would scream or something to call out to the panther.

A few minutes passes and I feel a sharp hit to belly and hear it fall and clatter into the logs and thatch at my feet. I don't know what it is, I do not see a thing through as the smoke thickens and fills my lungs with its poison. Another object strikes the wood next to my head, another grazes my cheek and I cannot help but cry out in pain. Others fall around me with little clinks.

"That's it, make her cry out! Make her summon the evil spirit animal in the woods. With her cry, he will come!" I hear the shaman call out to the villagers.

More objects are thrown, and I realize they are little pebbles being thrown at me. My people, the villagers, were throwing rocks at me. The shaman knew that I would not cry out I pain to summon the spirit animal, so he would have them hurt me before I died.

With my death, the shaman will keep his evil secrets. I do not think that it only intention is to see that Banu is banished.

Terror fills me as I see that amulet, the medallion around his neck pulse a sickly purple color and then the first bits of fire bite at me.

I look down, my eyes threatening to remain close from all the smoke and I see bright orange flames finally reaching me. The heat is unbearable and now with its proximity, I begin to feel the immense power of the fire, the heat. It does not yet burn me, but the heat hurts.

Panting, I cannot stop panting. My chest moving quickly—I cannot get my breath. Tears are streaming down my face; I cannot exhale normally. My breaths are coming out in coughs. My vision going in and out, darkness and light. My throat begins to seize up.

Sharps stabs of agony bite into my lower body as flames touch me. Stinging my flesh, burning.

A coolness, a blessed feeling, hits my face and runs down my body. Another splash of the gift of life hits me, other splashes onto the surrounding fires, cooling their touch. A thick mist rises around me as the fire is extinguished. Another splash drenches my head once again and as my hair trails down my face in watery rivulets, my eyes clear just for a second. I can see someone on top of the nearest shabono. Three figures.

My heart pains as I see Okalaki, my mama and my grandmama on the thatched roofs of the family homes. Tightly woven baskets have been gathered, their inseams dripping water. I cannot believe my eyes.

I can barely see anything. My lungs are heavy. Each breath thick and wheezy. Each inhalation is not enough. I can barely get one in before it came out sharply with a wet wheeze. I could not get a full breath. But I smile up at them letting them that I see them.

My mind feels fuzzy. My eyes are heavy. My chest is tight and thick. The edges of my vision are greying, tunneling close.

Shouts.

Cries of warning.

The people are yelling something. My eyes swam with shadows as my head lulls to the side. The growing darkness touches the corners of my vision and as I lifted my head to look, I think I see something.

There.

At the corner of the village. It moves too quickly for me to keep track of but when it stops, I think I recognize it.

Angry green eyes.

It is Banu!

When I recognize him, even as my thoughts blur, I see that he is not in his panther form. His fur remains on his body, his fingers tipped with thick black claws that glisten in SunFather's light. His once sleep black hair now stands on end, looking like an untamed wild mane.

His eyes flash the green eyes of the forest cat.

Hurriedly, people step away from him, out of his path that lead him towards the pyre. He is very tall, the tallest of the tall. Much taller than my father or the traders. His muscles of his thighs ripple with each of his steps, his hands stiffly at the sides, his claws unsheathing and sheathing, ready to kill. I notice a knife glinting in the SunFather's light between his fingers.

A sneer wretches my father's face as he turns and confronts Banu, stepping forward. His head is tilted back as he stares down his nose. "You cannot have the spirit walker!"

Zakopelli steps up to my father with a hand resting on his shoulder.

"Step back. You cannot fight this creature. He is mine." He thrusts the staff out, a wall of dust flies, and people drop where they have stood.

"No!" I scream but my voice is dry as my throat cracks and swells as if it is bled. The people, my people—no matter how much they have shown their hatred to me—I cringe as they fall still.

"You cannot help him now, Ara Macao," Zakopelli says, moving his staff threateningly just as my father does something surprising.

"Look at the evil magic he poses! Let me handle this!" He

shoved the old man backwards, towards the pyre, uncaring whether the shaman would have landed into the hot logs. My father does not look, he does not seem to care.

"So, you are the forest boy. The one who has stolen my daughter from me!"

"And you must be the filth that calls himself her father," Banu growls.

"You think that you're tough just because you are an unbonded beast? Well then, come on boy show me what you got!"

Banu launches himself at my father. His movement is like black lightning. He is fast. So quick. His knife twirls in his fingers like how mine twirls the pebbles, with ease and competency, he slashes and cuts, but my father mimics his movement. He gets the better for my father, his hand maneuvers into a twirl, catching my father off guard, sprawling him on the ground behind him. That only lasts a second, my father is on his toes and his fingertips and on all fours he jumps for Banu's throat. My dearest friend is expecting it and moves to block the blow. They step over prone bodies as their battle continues. The shadows at their feet are that of beasts. The panther and the jaguar, claws out, fighting for dominance and supremacy.

"Look at them both," Zakopelli whispers in awe. "Look at their power. Such beasts. Such power. Power. It can be mine. It can be all mine."

I frown at him but a tug at my wrist catches my attention, I feel a hand on my leg, and I turn, weakly, to see my grandmama at my side. My eyes stare at her for a long moment, I feel like I am staring at a ghost, when has she gotten so much white hair?

"I am holding him at bay, child. My magic is keeping his magic from corrupting your mind."

"What—what… do… you… mean?" I choke out the words.

My grandma shakes her head as she cuts at the cords that bind me to the post. "You did not listen to me, child. You should have bonded the spirit animal. Your power would have been so much greater than his if you had done so. But do not worry, I have tricks of my own. He does not control us all."

"Grandmama," my voice breaks.

"Look at them fight!" Zakopelli roars as the jaguar bites the panther on the shoulder. My eyes are wide with fright for Banu. "Their power will be mine!"

"Do not listen to him, don't let him pull you into his words. His words are tainted with evil and—" she has not finished cutting my binds when her words were cut off, a man steps up to her side, holding her hands still from finishing their cut. It is Tuonko, Aba's mate. "I am sorry, Menoakiki. I cannot allow you to do this. Aiko would be angry with me. Zakopelli would be angry with me. Please forgive me, Wise One." And he yanks the knife from her age-spotted hands.

"Don't be a fool, Tuonko. You are a strong man—you will as strong as the village leader to fight the power of Zakopelli. Don't do this. You see and understand the evil of this village is not of this girl or of that spirit animal."

"I see a spirit walker whose spirit animal is fighting the village leader. losing the creatures mate, the daughter of our leader, will betray our leader's confidence. I am sorry Wise One."

"I think you are very foolish. I used to watch you as a

child. You were always a stupid boy. Your willy is bigger than the brain that is in your head."

My grandmama meets my eyes, they are filled regret and lost chances. Tears fall from her eyes. "Hope is not yet lost."

I smile at her, letting her know that it is all right. She has tried. That is all I could have ever asked for.

A roar from the village and my father flies over the prone bodies and smacks into a wall near the fire pit where people would gather around the shaman at night to hear the stories of the ancestors. His hand flops to the side: unconscious. Banu breathes heavily, his claws at his fingertips beginning to grow as he stares heatedly at the fallen man. He is readying to strike the man had been my father.

I watch in terror, not yet ready to see the man who had been called my father to be struck down. Despite the anger and hatred, the animosity he has for my father, he turns away from the man. And meets the eyes of the shaman.

The end part of the staff—the part of white crystals and dancing red and blue feathers—strikes Banu in the chest. Banu hunches over, a clawed hand grappling at his chest.

And Banu falls backwards.

The shaman takes a step forward. Standing over the forest boy. My spirit animal. Unbonded and untamed. He raised his staff, readying to strike.

"Forest walker—you are mine!" And he swings the black staff.

Okalaki jumps in front of the shaman, swinging woven baskets filled with hot stones from the campfires—her arms bulge beneath the weight and I see red-hot coals strike Zakopelli in the chest, his amulet at his throat bouncing into the air like a glimmering purple butterfly. She swings the other bag, and it hits the old man in the face, and she slides forward with the momentum of the weights on her arms, collides into the body of the shaman and like a whiff of smoke, she vanishes.

Zakopelli lands in a heap, his fingers still clutching the black staff in his hand. He does not move.

Banu suddenly rises, shaking his head in a daze. He stands over the shaman before kicking the staff from the old man's hands. He seconds he is at my side, his claws poised to fight.

"Will you be next, villager?" He asks Tuonko.

"No spirit," Tuonko says, taking a step back. And then he flees. Banu watches him, a curious gleam in his eyes and I imagine that his tail would be lashing the air with a temptation to give chase. His claws rake at the remaining cords that are keeping me tied to the post. Gently, he wraps them around my body, my back pressing against the wooden poll.

His lips are large as he smiles, revealing his white teeth. Then he kisses me. My free hand slides down his chest, to his strong muscles of his abdomen. "Oh, Banu."

"It seems like I am always saving you."

"My protector," I choke out, my lung still feel heavy with the smoke I had inhaled. He stares at me concerned, then his eyes blink rapidly.

"You must get out of the smoke," my grandmama says urgently. "Both of you, out of the smoke!"

From out of the corner of my eye, I see something; white, blue and red that sparkle in the air as it comes crashing down on the back of Banu's head. We are standing on the warm logs as he falls amongst the smoke that is still wafting up from the dying fire.

It is the shaman.

He has regained his feet and a look of triumph colors his face. His eyes light up as they land on me. "You've done it, girl. Special Ara Macao. Oh, and is that Menoakiki? Ah—yes it is." His eyes stare at grandmama, full of malice.

A knife trembles in the air as my grandmama raises it. "Take this Ara Macao."

"A knife? What are you going to do with a small little fruit cutting knife? You going to challenge me to a fight, Ara Macao?" Laughter erupts from the shaman. He is so full of arrogance that he does not realize that I do not need a knife to be a weapon—I am the weapon!

Carefully, I take the knife from her and then quickly throw it at the enemy. The shaman only has a split second to react as the point glints in the light and slams into his chest. He flies backwards, off of the pyre and onto the ground where a pool of pool wells up from the knife. It has sunken in hilt deep into the old man's chest.

"Everything is a weapon to a forest girl like me!" I snarl at his dying form.

In my triumph I do not notice that Banu still lays crumpled at my feet. He is still in his human form, the form that I have come to love. He does not seem to be moving. His chest does not rise or fall.

I look down, my eyes going wide. My knees crash into the still hot logs, and I cry out in anguish. Banu. Banu.

A terrible sound fills the air and I realize the wailing is coming from my lungs, my smoke-filled lungs. My eyes are only for Banu as I cling to his still form. That horrible echoes as my sobs briefly cut off as I kiss his shoulder, his arms, his chest and his cheek.

"Oh, Banu. Please get up." I beg him.

He does not move.

It is as if my world has finally ended.

22

My world has ended.

My hands rest of Banu's chest, willing him to breathe but to no avail. I hope to feel his strength pulsing in his chest, to feel the heartbeat and to know he would be waking at any second. He does not.

A knock to the head. An ordinary man might survive it. Banu should be standing at my side, pulling me into his strong arms, his hot body pressing into mine. Smothering me with kisses and leaving cool marks on my skin where he has pulled away from. Banu does not move.

A firm hand touches my shoulder and I need not look up to know that it is my grandmama. "Ara Macao, you still have time. You must act if you want to save him."

I look up at her, frowning, my face wet from tears, and stained with soot and smoke. "What do you mean? He is dead, can't you see? I cannot bring back the dead. His chest does not rise and fall. He is gone. My Banu is gone. The forest boy is gone."

I thought I would feel shocked at her touch and that of Banu all out in the open, my ordinary quirks seem to have left me momentarily as I do not care as she hugs me from behind. A gentle, comforting hugs. I feel her head shake and then she pulls away and nods towards the forest. "You must take him out of here. The fire and the smoke harm him. It harms you, too. You must remember the old stories."

I blink my eyes, feeling confused. The smoke. I blink my eyes again. Yes, smoke is still around me. My lungs can attest to that. I let out a wet wheeze, disgusted at how I sound. But can what my grandmama say be true? Could he still be alive? I look at her with hope blossoming in my chest. "Is it true? Can he still be alive?"

"You must take him from here, to the forest and far away. Bond with him. The hunters will awaken soon. Take Banu away and do not return until you have mastered the path of a spirit walker." If what she says is true, if Banu still lives, I know in my heart that I will never be returning.

I look around and my grandmama's right. The bodies all around us are still, even my father's body is still. They must still be in the trance. Everyone all around were unconscious. The shaman did not move. Where was this power coming from? My eyes widen as I realize that my grandmama's hair is not just white, but her entire body is glowing a soft pale brilliance.

"Grandmama, I do not understand. What is this?"

"The power of a spirit walker," she says to me.

"How do you do this? They do not move because of you."

"You need not understand. Not yet. Just go from here, take

Banu and go. I can only hold them all for just a couple of minutes. I am old and my power is no match for the strength of the shaman. He has too much magic—stolen from the people of this village."

"But, grandmama, I don't—"

"Go, Ara Macao! There is not enough time to speak!" Her arms tremble and I can see that she speaks the truth.

Suddenly my mama is at my side, her hand touches mine gently. I am so shocked to see her that I stare at her as if I have seen a ghost.

"Mama?" My eyes are wide, staring at her hand that touches me.

"Take him from here, Ara Macao. I will help you as much as I can. Take his arm. I will take that of his other."

"Wait, where is Okalaki? I saw her attack the shaman. Where has she gone?"

"There is no time for that!" Mama says.

"Both of you, go!" Grandmama shouts, a surge of strength booms from her, and I can feel the energy quiver with her struggle.

"Come, Ara Macao. We must be quick." Mama grabs hold of Banu's arm and I mimic her and slowly, we withdraw from the village center. As the last shabono is left behind, the smoke suddenly clears, my vision clears as if a fog has risen. SunFather's heat and light grows brighter and no longer dim.

"That is the last of my power," I hear grandmama's voice in my head. I look over at mama who nods her head.

"Thank you, mother," mama says. "Grandmama Menoakiki strength has failed. The others will begin to stir."

"You know of her magic?" I ask, struggling to pull Banu

down the hill without tripping. Grasses and shoots pull and brush at my legs, nearly causing me to stumble.

"Have strength, Ara Macao. Have strength for your spirit animal and for your mother and all the people of the village."

"I don't understand, mama. You know about grandmama? And yet…"

"I do not have time to explain, I just hope you can forgive us all for keeping the truth from you. You are about to come into a great power, Ara Macao."

"What do you mean, power?"

"It is of our way. I have never used my magic—your father forbid me and in keeping my promise, he did not tell the shaman of the women's secrets."

"The women's secrets?"

"The women of the village have kept a secret for a very long time, in order to protect ourselves."

"To protect everyone, you all used me. Abused me."

"I am sorry, Ara Macao. You have a very strong spirit animal —one that needs bonding but not a forced bonding. You are different. You are special."

"That is what the shaman says, too. Then he tries to kill me. You all were going to let it happen," I growl through my teeth, not looking at her. Feeling hatred in myself for being grateful in her debt. I could not pull Banu by myself.

"The shaman is right," mama says. "You are very different and very special. It is why we keep things from you. You are the last of the peoples. The last spirit walker outside of your grandmama. She is too old; her magic and strength grow weak. You are the last."

I stare at her and wonder. What does she mean? My face

must've given away my confusion, my head pounds with each steps and I cannot help the drag of my legs. Mama does not seem to notice.

"Your forest boy is severely injured. He will die from the smoke if we cannot get him to the sacred springs. He must be taken from here. We do not have time to talk."

As we neared the forest edge, I heard a commotion from back in the village and mama looks frightened. She glances at me, the whites of her eyes wide in her eyes. "You must take him now. I cannot go with you. I must stall them."

"I don't know what to do. Where to go."

"Go to the spring of life. Go with him now. Drag him from here. Taken as far away as you can. I will try to stop anybody that comes."

My lungs barely have recovered as the full weight of Banu is under my arms. "Mama, I love you. Thank you."

"I love you too, daughter."

We pass my hut, the tree of the forest tall overhead, whispering their familiar hush to me. As I pull Banu into the forest, leaving the SunFather's light to the cool shade of the forest I see his chest begin to rise.

Hope blossoms in me with that gentle movement of his chest. I smile down at him. Oh, Banu. You were my protector for all of my life and now it is my turn to protect you. But I am not yet done. "Mama says the pool of life, but I do not know where that is. We need to get you out of here. Grandmama says far away. Maybe to the river? To our cliff?" Would that be far enough?

His eyes move beneath their lids, flickering and then blinking rapidly. Then he stares up at the forest canopy high above us as I drag him backwards into the forest. I glance up at the village, worried to be followed, but all is still in that direction.

He his eyes meet mine. And then he smiles at me.

"My spirit walker," he says to me.

"No," I shake my head at him. "You are the spirit walker. I am just a foolish girl."

"We are bonded. You and me. I the spirit animal. You the walker. See? You are walking." My smile widens with his words and he grows quiet. "Does this make you my mate?"

"I don't know," I say, worried at the silence coming from the village. "Be quiet. I am happy you are alive, happy you can speak, but keep quiet."

"The pool will heal us both, remember it? I wanted to take you there to swim."

I frown at him. Puzzled. Before I could answer his mouth begins to move again.

"You are a spirit walker. My spirit walker."

"Well if I am a spirit walker, then you are one too. Whatever the title means."

He smiles at me. "Yes, but you are the spirit walker. And we can make whatever we want of the title. At the pool. You and me. We must get there." His last words coming out breathy as if he is having trouble breathing, as I.

I stare down at him, unsure of what he means. He might still be delusional from all the smoke. I am surprised at my strength. For I have breathed in a lot of smoke. My chest still feels heavy. My temples still throb.

"If I'm the spirit walker," I finally say through pants. "What does that make you? My companion?"

"I am your mate," he growls fervently.

He rises to my cheeks and I am not sure if it's from the exertion of dragging a man twice my size. *Oh Banu.* "Yes, maybe you are my mate. For you were the first male to come in the village after all."

His crunches into a frown and then widen with delight. "You are right."

"Can you ever forgive me?"

I grunt. "If you shut up, I might be able to."

"For leaving you. Please forgive me. His magic vanquished me. I had many miles to run back here."

I look at him quizzically but don't say anything. My vision begins to edge with black again. "It hurt when you left. Hurt more than the physical pain of being assaulted. Hurt more than the hatred I have felt from my people. From the shaman. Hurt so bad but during my time, all I could think about is you."

"I'm sorry Ara. Please, I'll never leave you again. I'll—"

"Don't make promises you cannot keep. There will... always... be a time when you might not be able... to keep them."

"How can I make it right?" He asks.

By getting up and walking, I want to say. "Tell me you love me."

"What?"

"Tell me you will have me forever. Be mine, forever. Tell me you love me."

A gentle smile spreads across his face, "I—"

A flash of purple light consumed sight, within the glow there is a white light, dancing blue and red colors as a streak of power hits Banu in the chest, his arms are wrenched from my grasps as I am flung backwards with the force of the power. I roll on the grass, hitting a fallen log. On my elbows and knees, I raise my head, confused.

Banu is gone.

Where he was at stands the shaman. Zakopelli. His staff hits the ground and a thunderclap roars above me. The quakes. A large smile forms on his face and all I can see on his features is his wide smile of triumph.

His eyes hold no color, as the entire pupil dilates to cover his entire socket. As he stares down at me, I see flashes of embers in high evil sights. "Thank you for the spirit animal." His chuckle is low and ruthless. Dark and ominous. "You do not understand how long I have been waiting for that creature to be summoned by one of the women in the village or to bond with one of the boy hunters. I have waited, I have hoped for this moment for all of my life. You, my dear, have given me a wonderful gift."

"No!" It cannot be true. It just cannot be. We were almost away from the village. My strength, the last of my strength leaves me and I fall to my knees. I didn't want anything to do with that village ever again. I just want to leave and be with my friend. We were on our way out. No. No. No!

I scream and rise above the ground, an energy overtaking. My heart threatens to burst inside of me, a fire burning in my chest. Power bursts through my lungs and everything turn a brilliant white.

"What is that? No! No, it cannot be. You shouldn't be able to do that. No—No!" And the shaman disappears. I do not care. I think I have killed him but that does not satisfy me. Banu is nowhere to be seen. He is gone. I do not even have the corpse of the shaman for retribution.

I fall to my battered knees as the world fades. My arms hurt, muscles deprived of oxygen, are sore. The wounds that were once healing feel torn. Tears slide down my face.

I have failed. Banu is gone.

Gentle footsteps like falling feathers step up to my side. I look up to see that it is my grandmama. Her white hair no longer holding magic has fallen down and around her solemn face. "He is no longer here."

I nod. "Where did he go? What has happened to him?"

"The shaman vanquished him."

"I do not understand. I will never understand any of this." A rock is in my fingers and I have the sudden urge to throw it.

"I wish I had spoken to you, a long time ago child. But there have been hope that maybe you would have learned of these things on your own. It is not safe for women right now to have this knowledge openly. And you have always been special."

"Special, special, special. Quit calling me that."

"I am sorry Ara Macao. You were born different, and it was not safe to tell you things that you may accidently say to the shaman. We have kept many secrets from you. Your mother has tried so hard to keep the secret hidden, always so frightful that your father would tell the shaman. He has always been too close to the shaman. But the promise bound him to keep the secret for so long as your mother kept her promise."

"His body is gone! I don't know what's going on!"

"Child, you are a spirit walker. The shaman is a spirit walker. I am a spirit walker."

"You lie. Spirit walkers are evil. Remember? That is what I was taught as a child."

"The shaman's words. None of the women truly believe those things."

"Then why did you all keep it from me?"

Grandmama sighs and looks down at her fingers. "He was always watching us. You were always one to be outspoken and verbal when in the village. It is why we allowed you to roam freely in the woods. We knew the shadow cat watched you and he would never allow harm to you. Away from the village you were safest. For the shaman was waiting for someone to claim the spirit cat. Never did he expect it would be you. For you are different."

"You are a spirit walker. I remember our conversation by the river. But why did you never tell me? Okalaki hinted at it in the wigwam but still, she kept things from me too. I have been alone for so long and yet you are like me? The other women are like me."

"You are and will always be special. You are not just my granddaughter; you are gifted powerful magic. And with the bond to the shadow cat you will become immensely more powerful. You will overthrow the shaman for he binds the village to him in ways that you would not understand."

"Why would I understand when everyone keeps everything from me?"

"It is too much to say, with too little time."

I scoff. "And you said Zakopelli is a spirit walker? What animal is his bonded pair?"

"I have never figured that out child. And before you ask, mine is a secret for the shaman must never find out."

"You keep too many secrets from me!"

"With this secret, I am the only one protecting the village from becoming completely mindless slaves to Zakopelli."

"Grandmama, this is not a game. Banu's gone. The least I deserve is some answers and what am I supposed to do now? Banu is gone. I have no one. I am without a purpose."

"Don't be foolish, child. Use your brain. Surely in your forest boy, he has shown you a place in the woods that none else go. A place that merges our world with that of the spirit. I think you know of it all."

"What?"

"Think child. A place he must have brought you or wanted to bring you to."

"The spring?"

"Good, you know of the place. Do you know where it is?"

I nod.

"There is not much I can say right now. There's too much to say. If you wish to see the black panther again, you must go to the spirit world and retrieve him."

"The spirit world?"

"It is where he would have been vanquished to. No doubt your magic flung Zakopelli to the same place by mistake or perhaps during the moment of power I sensed coming from you, his spirit guide took him from danger to the place of the dead."

"What is my magic?"

"It is this thing of old. There is so little time, Ara Macao. I can tell you but the time ticks away for you to save Banu. If Zakopelli is in the fathomless void of the stars, then Banu is in grave danger."

"Why?"

"Without you he is not as powerful. You must go to him before he is gone forever."

"Gone forever? How do you know any of this tell me grandmama?

Grandmama shakes her head. "So little time and all you do is ask questions. Ara Macao, you must leave, immediately. Go and save him. Save him to save us all!"

"But what am I supposed to do. I do not know what I am supposed to do!"

"Open your hands," grandmama Menoakiki says to me. "See, look at that. The ancestors are already watching over you."

In my palms is the round rock, the rock that the shaman had noticed earlier, the rock that I had grabbed when I had fallen to the ground. It is in my palms, SunFather's gentle glow shining off it, giving it a blinding white color. My grandma took my hand into hers with very aged fingers and places a tiny finger stone. The rock is an ancestry stone, the kind I like to twirl in my fingers when in a fit of my quirks.

"Walk into the center of the pool. Be very careful not to let the rock touch the water until you are at the center. Fill water in one hand, while the rock is in another. And then you must, simultaneously, swallow both."

I nod my head vigorously. I would do anything to bring Banu back. To save him. To protect him as he has protected me. "Rock. Water. Swallow. I got it, grandmama."

I stand on shaking feet, clenching the white rock in my hand.

"Bring him back. And be careful, the spirit world isn't safe. It is a very dangerous place, Ara Macao. Do not let haste quicken your feet. Use your wits. Use your brains!"

"I will grandmama. Look after everybody in the village." I turn but hesitate, looking back at her. "Tell my sisters that I love them and that I love my mama. I wish them all the best." And then I ran. I ran before I could see the tears that fall from her face. I ran before I could see the fear in her eyes, before that fright hinders me on the path that I must go. I ran all the way up the path that I only knew.

Through the dense thick leaves of the forest, I bend at my waist, my feet smacking the moist ground of the forest floor. A glowing pool of light comes into my eyes at the center of the clearing and I know that I have reached the spring of spirits.

The holy water. The pool of life.

With the rock in my hand, I enter the water, my feet touching the cool spring water—it feels so good on my burns and the other hurts of my body. My hand is raised well above my head as I enter it. I wade to the center of the pool, careful to not allow the rock to touch the crystalline waters. My muscles feel relaxed and a healing energy buzzes throughout my body and I wish I had a moment to lay back in the pool and take it all in with Banu at my side.

With one hand, I cup of some water, with the other the rock.

Well, I think to myself. *It is now or never. For Banu!*

Water splashes my face and into my mouth as pebble hits my tongue and I swallow. The world around me lit up by a green fire, a cloud formed high above me in the blue sky, a cloud of stars, a cloud of cosmos. And then it rains upon my flesh, a cool, ethereal feeling splashing against my being, cleansing me of everything.

The world dims. The rains stops. The water drains beneath my feet. Glowing butterflies flew in front of me as I blink my eyes. The shadows danced and played. Bright purple flowers swayed in the gentle breeze.

I take my first step out from the spring of life and step into the world of spirits.

The End

ABOUT THE AUTHOR

Jess M. Rose is an emerging author of The Wilds novels and Spirit of the Ancients book series.